Weeping Woman

❖ *La Llorona and Other Stories*

Bilingual Press/Editorial Bilingüe

General Editor
    Gary D. Keller

Managing Editor
    Karen S. Van Hooft

Associate Editors
    Ann Waggoner Aken
    Theresa Hannon

Assistant Editor
    Linda St. George Thurston

Editorial Consultants
    Barbara Firoozye
    David Koen

Editorial Board
    Juan Goytisolo
    Francisco Jiménez
    Eduardo Rivera
    Severo Sarduy
    Mario Vargas Llosa

Address:
Bilingual Press
Hispanic Research Center
Arizona State University
Box 872702
Tempe, Arizona 85287-2702
(602) 965-3867

Weeping Woman

✤ *La Llorona and Other Stories*

Alma Luz Villanueva

Bilingual Press/Editorial Bilingüe
TEMPE, ARIZONA

ISBN 0-927534-38-X

Library of Congress Cataloging-in-Publication Data

Villanueva, Alma, 1944-
     Weeping woman : La llorona and other stories / by Alma Luz
Villanueva.
          p. cm.
     ISBN 0-927534-38-X (paper)
     I. Title. II. Title: Llorona and other stories.
PS3572.I354W44   1993
813'54—dc20   93-29735
                                                           CIP

PRINTED IN THE UNITED STATES OF AMERICA

Cover design by Kerry Curtis
Cover art Weeping Woman by Carmen León
Back cover photo by W. Q. Castaño

Acknowledgments

Major new marketing initiatives have been made possible by the Lila Wallace-Reader's Digest Literary Publishers Marketing Development Program, funded through a grant to the Council of Literary Magazines and Presses.

Funding provided by a grant from the National Endowment for the Arts in Washington, D.C., a Federal agency.

The quotation on pages 144-145 is from Upstairs in the Garden: Poems Selected and New 1968-1988 by Robin Morgan. Copyright © 1990 by W.W. Norton and Company.

Editor's Note

At the request of the author, we have respected certain idiosyncratic and dialectical variants in her writing.

❖ CONTENTS

To my daughter, Antoinette Villanueva,
who dreamt La Llorona years ago, in the rain,
scooping the world's tears with her black lace shawl.

❖ La Llorona/Weeping Woman

(All conversation between the child, Luna, and her grandmother, Isidra, is in Spanish.)

Luna looked out the rain-streaked window with sadness and boredom at the wet, gray street. "Will it ever stop raining, Mamacita? I hate the rain." Her voice was a murmur, fogging a small patch of glass in front of her. Luna was seven years old, and she resented being locked in with her grandmother for the third day. Her brand-new roller skates that allowed her to skate to the end of the block stood in a dark corner by the front door of the chilly flat. Only the kitchen was truly warm, where her grandmother stood rolling out handmade tortillas and a huge pot of beans simmered on the stove, sealed with fresh onions, fresh tomatoes, ground beef, cilantro, and a whole, bright red chorizo.

"If it keeps raining this way the water will rise, Niña. It'll rise up to the windows, maybe more." The old woman's dark face looked down at her dark hands rolling the white flour in perfect circles without any expression, though a faint, extremely faint, humor reflected, briefly, as a pinpoint of light in her large, dark Indian eyes that seemed to take in all light like a sponge. Like the Earth.

"Do you mean we could float away? Like a flood?" Luna's voice rose with excitement and fear.

"San Francisco is surrounded by water. The great ocean on one side, no? If it continues to rain this way, why not?" She walked over to the hot griddle and placed a perfect tortilla on it and flipped it by hand as gentle bubbles appeared on its floury surface.

"Are you scared, Mamacita?" Luna managed to ask. Where the day had been boring, watching the endless rain, now each drop was a threat, and it terrified her to think of the wild ocean getting closer. And if her grandmother was so calm, that meant there was no escape.

"If I were to hear La Llorona crying, then I'd be afraid, Niña."

Luna's eyes flew open and her small, pink mouth opened slightly, but she couldn't speak.

"All my life, in Mexico—" the child in front of her disappeared, and, instead, the old woman, Isidra, saw the stark desert landscape running, running to meet the wide, cool river, the cactus, the flowers, the birds, bright and plentiful, she could hear them singing—"when it rained too long, we could hear her, La Llorona, crying for her children down by the river. Crying and lamenting, with her beautiful black shawl over her head. Not for protection from the rain, no, but because she was either too beautiful, or perhaps too ugly, to behold."

A large yellow butterfly grazed her head, floating in the Sonoran heat, and Isidra remembered the tortillas. She placed the finished ones in a clean, worn towel, wrapping them tightly, and began rolling out a new white circle.

Normally, Luna would insist on a fresh, hot, buttered tortilla sprinkled with salt, but she was too absorbed by the image of a Weeping Woman who was too beautiful, or too ugly, to look at, and the rain was coming down, harder now, making the windows tremble as the wind in four loud gusts threatened the huge house, made into separate flats, with extinction. Only this kitchen is safe, Luna hoped. "Why was she crying, Mamacita?"

"For her children, Niña. When the great flood came, and the terrible men from the great ocean came, she turned her children into fish." Isidra paused to wet her dry lips. "It was the only way to save them," the old woman added, seeing the terror on her granddaughter's face.

"Were they fish forever?" Luna whispered. She imagined the house floating now out to the great ocean.

"When La Llorona cried like that, so loudly—" the old woman, Isidra, saw the river again; she longed to step in it, to touch it, to bathe—"they would come to her if her sorrow was so great. Then, she'd take the black shawl from her head, making sure no human being was nearby to witness her magic, and scooping it into the river like a net, her children would appear one by one."

The yellow butterfly, huge in the bright Sonoran sun, floated in front of her granddaughter, and Isidra thought of her three children who'd survived their infancy. The ones who'd lived long enough to hear about La Llorona. And then only one survived to adulthood: Luna's mother. May she not be like her mother, the old woman prayed for the child silently. I have no daughter, she added with her familiar sense of perpetual grief. Just the little fish the river took away, and I have no magic. No, not anymore.

The butterfly vanished into the chill San Francisco air and the child was speaking. "How many children did La Llorona have?"

"No one knows for certain, but, as far as I know, there were four like the four winds and all of them daughters. You see, Luna, she saved her daughters from the terrible men, but her sons stayed and fought and died. They were real Indians then, and the gringos just looked like plucked chickens to them." She began to laugh softly, revealing strong, square teeth. "The Indians knew they were evil when they killed even the little children for nothing, sending them to the dark side of the moon, so that the mothers couldn't even see their little ones in the Full Moon Face. Evil!" she spat.

"Why does it scare you, Mamacita, to hear her crying? Is she crying now? Can you hear her now, Mamacita?" The child drew up to her grandmother, resting herself against that fragile strength. Her grandmother.

Isidra rarely touched the child. That's the way she'd been brought up. After infancy she was rarely touched or pampered. But this was her granddaughter and who would know, she mused, as she smoothed the thick, curling hair from the child's wondering, frightened eyes. She looks like my mother, she thought. The same eyes. The same kind of pride and something ancient like mi mamá.

"No, Niña, I don't hear her now, but if I did I'd be prepared to leave this place because if her children will not be scooped into her shawl, La Llorona kills as many people as she can. Mostly men, but one never knows." Isidra squeezed the child once with her left arm and gently pushed her away.

"I don't blame her. She has her reasons to be so angry, and she has every reason to weep." The old woman sighed deep in her belly, in her old worn-out womb. "Since coming to this country," now she spoke in a low, secretive voice, "I have yet to hear her." Her eyes watered.

Quickly, she reached up and adjusted her red headband, the one she always wore in the house, but never, ever, in the street. Then, the old woman stiffened her body and spit into the air: "Too many gringos here,

3

mi Luna, and no room for La Llorona. No, no, she'll have nothing to do with them. Nor I."

In one swift movement she undid the towel, took a warm tortilla from the stack, buttered and salted it, and handed it to the child.

It was delicious, and the beans smelled wonderfully good now, and the rain outside seemed sad but bearable. "Do you miss La Llorona sometimes, Mamacita? She sounds awful, but I think I like her." Luna paused, glancing at the rain. "A little bit."

"What a question! Who could miss La Llorona?" Isidra laughed to herself. "Let's just hope you never hear her. But if you do, prepare yourself, Niña."

Luna's heart began to race again.

"Prepare to live or die. Yes, that's her message." As Isidra lifted the lid from the simmering beans, the brilliant yellow butterfly melted into the palm of her hand. She smiled as she scooped the beans into a bowl and placed it in front of Luna. "Now eat, Niña. Eat it all."

Thunder struck in the distance and lightning flashed, turning the kitchen window white with light, but Luna couldn't hear La Llorona. She ate without speaking, listening for the sounds of her unspeakable grief.

In the middle of the night, Luna woke to the loud voices. She froze, upright, in her bed, looking over to her grandmother's. Then she heard her grandmother's voice: "Don't treat me this way, Carmen, God will punish you. Yes, God will punish you for this." Her voice held no emphasis or threat; it was like a lament, a pleading.

"Make the bed, vieja! I feed you and put up with you. Now, make the goddamned bed, do you hear me, vieja?"

"It's a sin what you're doing. It's a sin, making me make the bed for you and that man." Then her voice changed as it rose to her old fury: "You aren't a daughter of mine! My children are dead!"

Luna heard her grandmother cry out, and she ran into the dimly lit front room where her mother stood over her cowering grandmother, her fist raised again. Carmen's harsh red hair shone dully in the faint light, but her eyes were bright with violence—the kind of violence that maims, or kills, the vulnerable. The kind of violence that's forgotten how to love.

"Don't touch her or I'll kill you! I'll kill you if you touch her again! I'll kill you!" Luna screamed hysterically, grabbing onto her grandmother's arm. It was as fragile and soft as a child's.

4

"See what you've started? I should throw you out! Out in the street! Out in the street where you belong, with this brat!" Carmen shrieked, hating the sight of the two of them together. Together against her.

There was a knock at the door and a man's voice. "Hey, Carmen, are you in there?" The voice was low-pitched and impatient. He knocked again.

"Just a minute, Frank!" Instantly Carmen switched her fury to a false, feminine charm. She ran to the bathroom and hurriedly applied some bright red lipstick, checking her light-skinned makeup for streaks. She pushed back her hair in an angry gesture and ran to open the door.

"Go to bed, Niña, I'll be right there. Go to bed. Would you like some cinnamon chocolate? I'll bring you some." Isidra touched the child's shoulders, guiding her toward their bedroom, and then she went to start the milk, putting it on a low heat. It would be ready when she was finished changing the sheets.

Carmen was making the man comfortable as he handed her a bottle of wine. "Oh, I pay her room and board, some extra money, to watch the kid for me. Got to work day and night, you know," she laughed knowingly. "I found her through a friend. Just relax and I'll get some glasses, baby." Carmen bent over to kiss him, offering her breasts to him. He cupped one, hungrily, as she giggled. Then he cupped them both and squeezed them a little too hard, but she said nothing, bringing her teeth down to taste the bright red lipstick.

It was late afternoon and Luna knew her grandmother was looking for her and calling her. "LUNA!" she'd be shouting in a thin, high-pitched voice from the second-story kitchen window. "LUNA!" as though the moon would know where her granddaughter was. "LUNA!" she sang to the setting sun, but no child sang back. Some boys in the distance jeered her, laughing, "Luuunaaaa!"

Pat, Luna's older friend, had talked her into coming to the park. No one would know, she'd said. Pat swung as high as she could and leaped to the sand, screaming.

"Do you want me to get you started? Come on, I'll push you." Pat's face was flushed with excitement as she held the swing for Luna.

"What're you kids doing here so late?" a male voice said, interrupting their play. He was a teenager, but he looked like a man to the girls. They stared at him quietly.

"Don't you know it's against the law to be here this late?" He showed them a badge. "I'm a policeman and I'm going to have to take one of you in. I'm going to have to call your parents."

"She'll go!" Pat said, running down the cement path.

As the boy hurt Luna, he said, "If you scream, I'll kill you." She didn't scream or cry, but she did hear La Llorona weeping very close by.

"The hymen's intact, so he didn't rape her, and there's no trace of semen," the doctor told Luna's mother. Pat had run home, and Carmen was getting ready to go to her night job as a waitress. By the time Luna got home Carmen had called the police.

The doctor was hurting her again where the boy had put his finger, and she had to tell them about how he touched her everywhere. She looked at her mother, but she seemed only angry at the nuisance, as though Luna had staged everything to annoy her.

"So, she wasn't raped?" Carmen asked the doctor once more.

"There's no evidence of it."

"Well, nothing happened to you, Luna, so stop that trembling act. Do you hear me?"

"Excuse me," the doctor interjected, "she's been through quite an ordeal for a seven-year-old. She'll need to talk about it. . . ."

"Well, I don't have time for all that. As it is I'm late for work." Carmen rushed Luna into her coat, pulling on her to be quick.

"Here's the number for a *free* clinic." The doctor, an older woman, handed it to her, though she knew it was useless.

As Luna and her mother settled into their seats on the bus, Carmen told her, "Keep this to yourself. Nothing happened to you anyway, cry baby." She kept her voice low in the bus, but Luna heard the hatred anyway. "The old woman makes a big deal out of nothing as it is."

"Where are we going, Mamacita?" Luna asked, looking out the bus window at the beginning darkness and the rain blurring the streets going by. They never went out at night except to go to church once a week, and then someone always picked them up in their car and brought them back home. So, Luna had no idea where they were going.

"We're going to the great ocean." Isidra had her old, dark wool coat on and a plastic scarf over her head, her going-out dress, and many pairs of stockings to keep her legs warm, but her shoes, unsuited for the rain, were wet. The umbrella rested, closed, between them, dripping a long, thin puddle towards the feet in front.

"Why?" was all Luna could say. Isidra put her hand on top of Luna's small, cold hand. Years later, Luna would remember her grandmother's touch was like dry, loose feathers. Comfort without pain. Strange, irrational—*a silent comfort.*

Luna had to help her grandmother off the bus because the step to the street was so high and the driver hadn't pulled close enough to the curb. There was a fast food place a block from the beach. They entered the front door with fear and excitement. They rarely went out to eat. Luna told her grandmother the menu in Spanish and waited for her to decide. Some people came and got in front of them, but it didn't matter. Luna ordered in a shy, proud voice. No one paid the least bit of attention to them as they sat by themselves eating. And they hardly spoke as the rain came in gusts.

"Come, walk quickly, Niña," Isidra commanded, holding the umbrella up over their heads with her right hand and Luna with her left. They rushed across the street, as fast as they could go, to the roar.

It was absolutely dark now except for the flickering streetlight behind them. The immense white waves frothed at their peaks, a terrible darkness beneath them, and then, suddenly, in long, smooth lines, they'd decide to meet the earth, angrily, with their roars. Luna wanted to turn and run, she was so terrified, but her grandmother held her hand lightly. She looked up at her grandmother and her eyes looked far away as though she were straining to see something.

"There she is," Isidra hissed. "There she is!"

"Who?"

"You can't hear her because of the ocean, but there she is!" Isidra drew Luna close to her, feeling the smallness of her body. She felt the trembling stop.

There was a dark figure moving along the beach, slowly. Her shawl covered her head. She looked tall and strong as she came toward them, weeping and singing.

The Virgins ❖

"Do you have the business yet?" Eva asked July as they skipped down the
city street. It was a real spring day, and there wasn't a trace of fog or smog
to mar it. It was, in fact, the kind of day that told them secret things: that
they'd be beautiful when they grew up and probably famous or something.
Certainly, they'd be rich and never have to cook or do the hump or any of
that disgusting stuff they knew their mothers had to do just to survive.

July came to a halt. "No, do you? My mom says once you get it you're
like doomed. A man just has to look at you and you start swelling up,
you know?"

"Nah, me neither. My mom says once you get it, the business and all,
you start wanting to give it away." Eva laughed, trying to sound grown-up
like her mother. Instead, she just sounded like a scared kid.

July felt embarrassed for her friend and tried to cover up by saying,
"Yeah, my mom says that if she'd charged for all the times she gave it
away for love"—here she tried to laugh harshly with a proper scorn—"she'd
be a millionaire by now," but she succeeded in conveying only a secret
sadness. She couldn't call it shame, so it masqueraded as her own personal sadness as though it had nothing to do with her mother, as though
she'd been born that way, with her own personal sadness, with her name
on it. July tossed her head nervously in the warm sun as a fresh wind blew
her hair in her face. She had long, black hair, past her shoulders and when

she ran it streamed behind her, or slapped her in the face, making her look wild and free as an untamed horse.

Eva's hair was a dark auburn and short like a boy's, but frizzy and bushy. It was her eyes, a pale hazel-yellow, that made her look like a young, hungry wolf whether she was running as fast as she could, or standing, or sitting absolutely still. A cornered wolf. She sniffed the air, lifting her battered tennis shoes quickly, heel to toe, heel to toe, checking for readiness. For the spring, the leap. Escape.

"Last night when I got up to pee," Eva paused and gathered herself—then she continued in a deceptively dull tone, "she forgot to shut her door, and I saw this old guy on her. It looked like he was eating her thing, you know? Like his mouth was on her, and he was making noises like he was eating soup, and she was enjoying it. I could tell. And she always told me she did it only for the money so we can eat and all."

"I seen my mom doing it a bunch of times. She always looks like she's enjoying it, but she says she's got to look that way." July's voice was low. She'd never said this to anyone and somehow saying it made it real to her, as though for the first time, and now the beautiful sunshine, the perfect day, was beginning to feel too hot, oppressively hot, and the cracks in the broken cement sidewalk matched the cracks in her soul. She couldn't have said *soul* or even *heart*. It was suddenly just too hot and the skinny city trees gave no shade.

"I was thinking last night, if getting the business makes you like that, I think I'd rather die." Eva's voice rose slightly with anger and then dropped off again. "I mean, her eyes were closed and she was moaning like a sick hippo, like she was going to die or something." Eva started to giggle. "I mean, maybe *she* paid the old guy, you know?"

July giggled with her, relieved, in a strange way, to be laughing at their secret. They'd met in class and then visiting each other's flat made them comfortable with the other. They both had old furniture, dirty curtains, and nothing in the refrigerator. They ate mostly at the Taco Palace, where the tacos were pretty fresh and cheap. They put up with the old guys who hung out there, leering at them, murmuring, "Qué linda, chica. . . ." things like that. The younger guys pretty much left them alone, except for one guy who made ritual comments about July's cantaloupes, as he called them. Both of their mothers drank and did pills. Eva's older brother was dead. He'd fallen off a roof, they said, and he was the only person she ever loved or cried for. She didn't even cry for herself. She was over that.

Both of their fathers blended with the steady stream of men, the images of men, they'd seen, but Eva remembered her father, vaguely, and what she remembered only made her angry. Fists and shouts. Then the terrible silence of a crime and the soft sounds of wounded cries.

"One time this guy saw me getting ready for bed and before I could shut my door, he came inside. He smiled at me really ugly. My mom came in and he said, 'Is this kid for sale? She still a virgin?' 'No, the kid ain't for sale,' my mom said, and she forced herself to smile, but I could tell she was pissed off and all." July's voice trailed off, remembering the man's harsh sounds in her mother's bedroom down the hall. July had an okay bedroom, everything from the Salvation Army, and she had a real bed and a chipped-up bureau, but it had a huge mirror. July had gotten up out of her bed and stared into the mirror until the sounds in her mother's room stopped and the traffic below was allowed to continue all night. She'd sat there, staring into the mirror, and asked herself, over and over, Is the kid for sale?

July and Eva sat down on some sunny steps. They could hear a child crying somewhere in the building behind them, and it made them sad for no particular reason. They didn't know it was the beginnings of hopelessness.

"Are you a virgin?" Eva asked, staring at the line of ants marching back and forth from a crack in the cement. She wondered how deep the cement went and where it stopped, if it ever did. A little yellow flower had blossomed in the ants' crack. Eva picked it, twirling it around.

"Yeah, I guess so. Are you?" July sighed with disdain, watching the flower twirl in Eva's hand. It was a blur of yellow and then it'd stop and then Eva would twirl it again as the green stem began to bleed its sweet, translucent juices, making her fingers sticky.

"I guess so. This guy stuck his fingers in my you-know-what one time and it hurt so bad I kicked and bit him and ran out of the house. I was just eight, does that count?" Eva stared at the brilliant flower. She was sorry she'd picked it.

"Where was your mom?"

"Passed out. I hid behind a car till he left." Eva began twirling the flower again, blurring its yellow, left to right. "Do you think that counts? I mean, maybe I'm worth less now or something, you know?"

Secretly, July had always wondered how much that guy would've paid to buy her. How much? "If you don't have your business yet you must be worth a lot, I guess." July smiled.

"Put your chin up," Eva commanded, holding the yellow flower close to July's face. "Yeah, you're going to have lots and lots of boyfriends," Eva said with satisfaction, laughing high and shrill.

"How do you know?" July didn't laugh. In fact, she looked somber as though she'd been sentenced to death.

"Eva's eyes held a harsh, glassy malice. "Because if there's yellow on your chin, it means you're going to have *lots* of boyfriends."

"No, it doesn't!" July tried to grab the flower from Eva and missed. "Let's see if your chin gets yellow. Bet it's yellower than mine!"

Eva crushed the flower in her hand, feeling its soft petals squish. Then, angrily, she threw it in the oil-stained street. They sat in silence, and then a drunk stumbled by and offered them each a dollar, "Fer sm iiscream," he slurred, smiling. They grabbed the dollars and ran.

"Do you wanna go get an ice cream?" Eva asked sullenly, tracking July with her yellow-green eyes, watching her hair stream in the gusting air, freely.

"Yeah, why not. I'm hot," July said matter-of-factly, forgetting the flower and its omen.

As they passed a sloppy-looking building streaked with old pink paint, Eva remembered the time some kids had taken her upstairs. "They have dead bodies upstairs. The doctors cut them up. It's really gross." Eva smiled.

July regarded her friend like the first time they'd met—cautiously. "I don't believe it. Why should they have bodies in there, anyway?"

The yellow in Eva's eyes pierced the hazel background like slender, sharp darts. "Come on and I'll show you. Are you chicken? Come on! You have to be quiet, so don't talk!"

When they opened the door, it smelled like a school or something and it was absolutely silent.

"What if they're in there?" July whispered.

"It's Saturday! Shut up!" Eva turned her eyes, angrily, toward July, and July instinctively backed away.

The old wooden door had a latch and Eva slipped it open without a sound. Her skin had goose bumps as she opened the door.

July was holding her breath, but when she saw the head directly in front of her, her breath came out so sharply she almost screamed. There was a torso on one table, an entire body, head and all, on another. All the bodies were very white, except for the brown torso, and deader than dead. In the corner was the body of an old lady. Her legs were spread apart awkwardly,

11

and her face looked outraged. It smelled absolutely horrible, like everyone was being killed, again and again.

"I dare you to touch the old lady!" Eva said rather loudly, forcing herself to speak, sounding, she thought, a little like God, so alive among the dead.

"Why should I?" July could only whisper her reply.

"I touched a body when I came," Eva lied. "It's fun. Go on, touch her! She doesn't care!" Eva laughed, feeling proud of her new strength and power and the fear in July's eyes.

Forcing herself to walk, July stumbled on a cord as she crossed the room and, as she touched the old woman's flesh, on her fleshless belly, Eva shut the door behind her, latching it. As July turned at the sound of the latch, the old woman seemed to come to life, and the outrage stretched across her face turned to a grimace. *I am you*, she seemed to say to July.

July screamed an animal's fear, a pure fear, and she ran for the door, pulling on it. Finally, human words came to her: "Eva, Eva, please let me out! Please! Please, Eva!" July waited for the touch of the old woman on her shoulder, on her back. As July pulled frantically on the old wooden door, a clear, rational thought came to her: Did they buy the old woman or was she free?

Eva stood frozen on the stairs, afraid that July's screams would bring the doctors. She ran up to the door, unlocked it, and ran for the street. July was close behind her, panting and sobbing. Now the bright sun was terrible, making the pale dead more real to the girls.

"Why did you do that? Why?" July cringed at the touch still in her finger. Both of them ran down the block, away from the building.

"I don't know," Eva answered blankly, her strength and her power gone now among the living.

July raised her right fist, bringing it down hard on her own leg. She shook her hair back with a toss of her head. "You little whore!" The words seethed out of her. "You're not a virgin, so you're not worth a shit, that's what!"

Eva's shoulders slumped forward and almost under her breath she said, "You touched the old lady, you touched a dead person."

"That's because I'm brave, you little whore! Puta!" July laughed harshly and ran away at full speed.

There was nowhere for Eva to go. She never went home in the daytime if she could help it. She fingered the dollar in her pocket and she felt some sand and a chipped seashell still there from a field trip last week. She threw away the seashell and clutched the dollar tightly in her fist. Then for no reason, no reason at all, she began to cry.

There Was A Time ✣

He had no idea what he was searching for. He never really did. Mainly, he liked the general chaos of old things thrown in boxes: dresses for little girls, pants and shirts for little boys, shoes tied to each other, some not—scuffed and used from endless play. Running, running, yes, he could see a group of children of various sizes running, screaming, and laughing. One fell, crying, a hole in the knee. He put his finger through it and smiled.

He looked through a box of cooking utensils, most of them scraped and battered but still very usable. He took everything out, looking to the bottom, and found a large wooden spoon, almost like new. Also, a wine cork stained red. He smelled it: nothing. He put it in his pocket. Maybe he'd pay for it, maybe not. He put the wooden spoon in his jacket pocket. He'd pay for the spoon, no question.

Now for the women's clothes. He pulled each one out from the rack, fingering the material, imagining a different woman inside each dress. Or at least he thought so because each one had different colored hair as he looked at her, but the face remained the same. It was his wife, but he hadn't seen her in over forty years. He'd just walked out one morning and never returned. Her and the three kids.

"Are you looking for something for your wife?" a very young saleswoman asked. She was tall and blonde and she looked amused.

"Yes," he lied, smiling back at her. "But she doesn't like anything I buy her, so I gave up a long time ago. She does like this color though." He spread the skirt of a slightly faded cotton turquoise. "It's her favorite color all right." He told the truth this time. Briefly, he wondered if she still liked turquoise anymore.

"Is she a size fourteen?" The woman brought the dress out, turning it around. "The zipper works, too. See?" She pulled the zipper up and down, looking at the old man. He was casually dressed, with a slightly dignified air about him. He stared at her, not the dress.

She asked again, "Is she a fourteen?"

He looked quickly at the dress, trying to imagine his wife forty years ago. "No, she's smaller, I think." He looked back at the saleswoman. "She's shorter than you, that's for sure."

"I see." She put the dress against herself. "It's long for me." Then she hung it back, smiling at the old man. "Let me know if I can help you, okay?" she offered, going back to sorting clothes out of a box on the other side of the room.

"I will, thank you." He tugged at the hem of the turquoise material.

"Maybe she should come in and try some things on. That's the only way to go." The woman's voice was automatically cheerful, distracted. Her date still hadn't called, and he'd promised. Especially after last night, the first time and all. I should know better by now, she thought angrily. You have to let them dangle for months. Months, the word echoed in her mind, in her mother's voice, making her feel utterly stupid. Helpless. The very first night. Stupid. Stupid. Stupid.

The old man's words interrupted her silent tirade. There was no one else in the store. Rain all day and almost closing time. And no call.

"My old lady wouldn't be caught dead in a secondhand store. Thinks she's too high class and all. Rather wear a new thing to death, that woman. And always the best shoes for the kids." He looked at the young woman as she continued to sort the box of clothes. He pulled the faded turquoise zipper up and down, slowly.

"You have kids?" She glanced at the phone as if it might be ringing and if she looked at it, it would come to life.

"They're grown up now. Two boys and a girl." His voice trailed off as he tucked the dress back with the others.

She smiled at him. "Do you have grandchildren?" Now, here's a man who's been with the same woman for years, who stuck it out, she thought.

He smiled back. "Too many, too many."

"Why don't you look in the toy section. Maybe there's something in there for them." She glanced at the phone again, then at the clock tacked onto the dusty off-white wall. Tomorrow, she promised herself, I'll go see about a boutique job, selling new stuff, maybe men's clothes. Meet some new men. Manager of a secondhand store. Used goods. She sighed. Suddenly, she wanted to cry long and loud to her fill, to the full extent of her self-pity.

He walked over to the toy section and fingered the toys. Most of them were faded, broken, or about to break. He had a good pension. He could send new toys if he wanted. To who? he asked himself. And where?

"I'm closing in about ten minutes. We open in the morning at nine-thirty if you want to come back." But I won't be here tomorrow, she reminded herself. No, not tomorrow.

He browsed through the neighborhood secondhand store about twice a month. Tomorrow would be too soon to come again. This is when he thought of them—the wife, the kids—though he didn't know this. This was when he visited them. It was as though they had worn these dresses, these pants and had cooked with these pots, stirred with these spoons, read these books, worn the various sized shoes. He imagined he knew them by touching these discarded items.

The phone rang and she ran to it, knocking over a display of cheap, uninteresting jewelry. The kind that made you wonder who'd buy it in the first place. The kind that made you laugh, then cry.

"Yes," she said. "You have to be here to open by nine. Yes. Bye." She looked at the box of clothing, half sorted, and decided to leave it that way. I need a drink, she thought. Immediately.

"I'm closing now," she called out to the old man.

"Be right with you," he answered. A small cardboard box of seashells caught his eye, and he rummaged through it briefly. They weren't the perfect, polished type usually found for sale, but the worn, unpolished type usually found while walking along the beach. He shook one and sand came out, scattering on the floor. He picked up the box of shells and the fine sand crunched under his feet.

He often walked along the shore, at least three or four times a week. He was so close to it and walking kept him in shape. But he never collected shells. In fact, he had never stopped to pick one up and stare at it. At the design, the coloration, the message of time and tide and such things. No, he walked and walked, looking out to the waves and up to the clouds occasionally. But, actually, he didn't really see the waves or the clouds. They were just something that had to be out there. Something to be tolerated because it existed.

"Is that about it?" the woman asked, indicating the box in his hands.

"Oh, also this wooden spoon." The old man handed it to her.

"Do you collect shells?"

"Off and on."

"Well, these aren't the shiny type. You like them this way?" She looked into his dark, humorous eyes.

He remembered the wine cork in his pocket and fingered it. "Saves me the trouble, young lady." He smiled at her and his finely-trimmed mustache moved up at the corners. He could be so charming. People liked him, and he had his morning buddies where he almost always ate breakfast. But he preferred loneliness and silence like a comforting fog that shrouded him, giving him complete privacy. Failure and success no longer hunted him. No one knew if he was a failure or a success, therefore, he himself didn't know.

"Look, I'll charge you for the spoon. How's twenty-five cents? Keep the shells, on the house." She took his quarter.

"Well, I thank you."

She looked at him as his smile revealed small, white teeth. It'd be nice to have a father like that. "Want to go have a drink? A glass of wine or something?" The words tumbled out of her, expectantly.

He looked pleased and flattered, but already her voice was irritating him. Women's voices had always gotten on his nerves. Only his grandmother's voice—low, modulated words sought out, chosen carefully like a secret—had held him captive as a child as he listened to her tell him stories about how things had been. Everyone else considered it nonsense, a waste of time. But not the boy, waiting for the old woman to decide to talk. She would fasten her eyes on him and he would look at her with his full attention, and then she'd begin as her fingers moved, sewing.

"A shame you aren't a girl so I could teach you something useful," his grandmother'd said harshly, indicating the bundle of cloth in her lap. The boy would say nothing. Even smiling might make her change her mind. He'd just look up at her and then she'd begin with her usual sigh of subtle failure, "There was a time, you know . . ." and she never looked at him again, but at a far-off place only she could see. She might glance at him once or twice, sighing again.

He looked at the young woman, at her hazel eyes waiting for his reply. "I'd love to, dear, but my old lady would surely kill me with dinner waiting at five-thirty. Promptly, you know." The cork in his hand felt lovely.

Disappointment flickered in the dark hazel eyes. "Oh, I understand. Of course, it's your daily commitment. How nice. Have you been married long? Well, of course, you have," she caught herself, laughing.

"Yes, a long, long time," he lied. "Have a good evening," he added as he opened the door to leave.

"I will," she lied, locking it and turning the OPEN sign to CLOSED. She imagined his wife, small and stern, waiting for him with a warm meal on the stove. Maybe she's wearing a turquoise dress, new of course, the woman thought sadly. Maybe I'll find someone like him. The thought comforted her.

The sky was clear this morning as the old man watched the spectacular white clouds move with the force of the wind. He never imagined them to be anything; he just liked to see them move. He wondered if any of his old customers at the post office asked where he was. He wondered if the coffee maker was broken again. If they'd replaced it. He sipped his coffee slowly. He turned on the radio, but the voices bothered him.

He looked at the forlorn box of sea-worn shells and picked one up. It was small and chipped, but in the morning light patches of rainbows shone, subtly. He picked up another. It was larger and not chipped at all. He followed the monotonous spiral design with his eyes to its bluish conical tip. Then he saw traces of little rainbows in the spiral's grooves.

He picked up a fragment of abalone and turned it in the clear morning light. Bright pinks and blues glared at him. He put it down. "Retirement," he said out loud. "Useless old bastard." He finished his coffee and his stomach began to growl with hunger.

The ocean was turbulent, spraying salt in every direction, and the old man walked on the hard sand close to the tideline, being careful not to get wet. The sun shone through, fiercely, for a moment, and the spray of the tide cupped a series of curled, brief rainbows.

He saw a child up ahead walking toward him with what appeared to be his mother. The child—he couldn't tell if it was a boy or a girl—kept running into the waves, screaming, and back to its mother, grabbing her in sudden rapture.

Quickly, he took the box out of the plastic bag. He almost put the box down on the sand with the shells piled inside one on the other. It won't look natural, he thought, correcting himself. He flung them, not widely, but close together. He put the box back in the plastic bag and walked on.

The child and the woman passed him. The child's eyes met his, briefly, full of mischievous laughter, and then he ran back to the sea with his arms spread wide, screaming.

The old man looked back and saw the woman bent, staring at the sand. The child joined her. The child immediately began to collect the shells, placing them in his jacket pocket.

"Save some for some other children, why don't you?" his mother laughed. But she meant it. She wished he would.

"They're mine! I found them! They're mine!" he whined loudly, threatening to cry, holding a piece of abalone in his hand.

The old man walked on to the deserted end of the beach where he always rested. His stomach loudly protested its lack of food as he sat on his usual rock looking out at the sea. Today he really looked; he saw its heave and spray; and he heard it. Usually, he rested for a few minutes, letting the sea be where it was and what it was: a great massive wetness with no real use. To him, anyway. He wasn't a fisherman or a sailor and he rarely ate fish and he never learned to swim as a child. His father had drowned crossing a river, showing off, his mother'd said. "A big, strong man like that, just washed away like a leaf. Like a leaf." She'd never spoken about him again after she'd married the new man. She'd never let him near the water. The new man had called him a *sissy* and slapped him for crying. Sometimes he beat him with a belt and did other things he refused, even now, to remember.

He'd run away at fourteen, nearly starving, doing odd jobs. Then a bootlegger hired him to do errands, and he got slightly rich. The bootlegger was big and strong and he laughed a lot, especially at the awkward boy, almost man. Then the bootlegger was killed in a fight one night when he was drinking, and the boy, almost man, lied about his age and went into the army. He'd fooled them all. He looked big and strong, just like a man. Not a leaf, a man.

The ocean was singing to him now in a low, modulated voice. If only his stomach would stop growling he could hear it better. He stood up, feeling his knees ache at the sudden motion.

"Old man, old man," he muttered, feeling his spine and the back of his legs complain. His mouth was dry from lack of food.

He walked toward the tide and the sea's singing was lower, louder—a thunderous, continuous sound. He saw a starfish at his feet. "Ugly creature," he greeted it. But he picked it up, shivering at its inhuman touch, and flung it out to the waves. He didn't know why he did it; he just had to, that's all.

He continued to walk toward the beautiful voice of the sea. His shoes were wet and now he was up to his knees. The sea sighed in a split second of silence, and, gathering her voice, she began, "There was a time, you know . . ."

✣ Place of the Dead

Occasionally bodies washed up, but she'd gotten used to it, almost as though it were the most natural thing on Earth that bodies should wash up to shore like seashells. She only glanced at them; they'd ceased to horrify her like they had in the beginning—their missing eyes, disfigured faces, open abdomens, everything dissolving, shredding, bloating, soundlessly, so peacefully, as they rocked in the waves.

The people from her village would come, periodically, and bury them, especially when a child's body washed up on the shore. The people would take the small body to their own cemetery, burying it in the name of innocence, in the name of the Virgin. She would comfort the little one, they knew. Then they'd go home, silently, and light the candles on their altars, praying to the Virgin to keep their own children safe from the Insane Ones. They prayed with all their hearts that the Insane Ones would never, ever return to their village: killing, raping, killing. Just for its own sake, their eyes hard, glassy, insane, laughing at the sounds of sheer, naked suffering, grief.

They'd left, the last time, leaving half the village dead, raping even many of the little ones and killing them for their final, ultimate pleasure. And then, two or three of the Insane Ones, not able to restrain themselves, had violated the small dead bodies. Only death could satisfy the Insane Ones. Only death itself.

They'd buried these little ones with particular care, handling them gently. The mothers the Insane Ones had left behind had swallowed their souls, so their grief was terrible and mute. The dead mothers joined their castrated and murdered husbands, their dead children, and were safely beyond human grief. And some of the young mothers, and the young childless women, had been taken.

The child didn't know her mother for she'd been one of the women taken. She and her grandmother had hidden in the corner behind the harvested corn. When one of the Insane Ones came to find the food, he saw them; the old woman crouched down holding a sleeping baby of a few months.

The old woman held her granddaughter tighter to her bony chest and moved her lips, imploring the Virgin. She stared at the Insane One, waiting to die.

"Kill us both," the old woman whispered.

This one was very young, maybe sixteen. He picked up the bulky sack of corn and a small sack of beans. His rifle banged her knees as he bent forward to lift the sacks.

"Kill us both," the old woman repeated, her eyes fixed on his for movement.

He placed the sacks down beside him and unshouldered his rifle. He looked at the old woman's tired eyes and the baby's quick, soft breath as she slept. The baby shuddered. He shouldered his rifle, angrily, picked up the sacks and said, "Light me a candle, abuela," and for an instant his eyes looked like a boy's.

"Sí, hijo. May the Virgin watch over you." Her eyes had been grateful, but only for the child. And how would she keep this child now, with no milk? she asked herself. If only they don't find the goats, she begged the Virgin silently.

She heard the women screaming outside, the brutal male voices, and she wondered how the child could sleep. She must be blessed to be so quiet. But your mother, niña, is not blessed.

The old woman shut her eyes and listened to the screaming turn to moans and cries of grief. She knew the Insane Ones were gone. "May the Virgin watch over you, hija," she whispered to her beautiful, her only, daughter. She would never see her alive again, she knew.

The child had found a lot of useful things this morning. Sh̶
her grandmother could use an umbrella, a shiny spoon, a rusty
tennis shoes from the dead woman's feet. Her grandmother wou
gry she had come to the shore again without her permission, but
knew her anger would be brief seeing the shoes. Even the other children
wouldn't come with her. They were afraid. So she came alone. Sometimes
the older boys would beat her to the treasures, but she always seemed to
find something.

A tin box was wedged into the sand tightly, so she squatted down and
dug it out. Finally, when she opened it she was disappointed. A bunch of
old, useless seashells were piled inside. She almost threw the shells away
to keep the tin box—That's useful, she said to herself—but then she decided to keep them for her grandmother. "Maybe for her altar," she said
out loud.

The old woman lit a candle every week for her daughter and for the boy
who'd spared their lives. She'd adopted him, calling him hijo, the one who
was sane among the Insane Ones. "Just a boy," she'd say as she lit his
candle. When she lit her daughter's candle she was silent, like when she lit
the one candle for all her dead babies. The one for her mother and father,
silent, as the one for her husband. Silent. But for theirs, her own and her
granddaughter's, she'd whisper, "Keep us close to your heart, mi Virgin."

The child sifted through the box of shells and pulled out an intact, delicately hued, pink shell. It was tightly clamped and closed against all eyes.
She was tempted to pry it open; instead she shook it. A fine sand leaked
out. She held it up to the morning sun, but the shell revealed nothing. She
picked up the others, and though they were beautiful and whole and
hardly chipped at all, only this pink shell was closed against her, with its
secret safe inside.

She put this one in the hem of her dress and tied it into a tight little
knot. Then she picked up the other treasures, tying the shoe laces together and placed the large, wet tennis shoes around her neck. The rest
she juggled in her hands and arms. She'd walk her secret way back to the
village so the older boys wouldn't take anything from her. She began to
imagine her grandmother's face after she was through being angry with her
for coming to the shore. To the Place of the Dead. She saw her grandmother begin to smile as she untied the knot in the laces. And she'll love
the knife too, the child smiled to herself. We'll sharpen it and take away
the rust.

"I love the Place of the Dead," the little girl said out loud. And then she began to hum, to keep herself company, feeling her mother's gift—small and secret, perfect and whole, delicately pink and closed against her—bump gently against her leg as she walked, quickly, home.

✛ Real Rainbows

They were always after him to carry the stuff. They called out after him as he rode by, "Hey, little brother, make nuf ta feed yo mama for a month, boy! Hear me, boy?" Then they'd laugh loudly in his wake. "Buy yrself a bike, boy! Wit some fuckin wheels on it! Sheeeit!

He clutched the handlebars tighter, his face turning hot at the ridicule. His mother bought it for him at the secondhand store last year for his ninth birthday. "Ah'll get ya a new one, Sonny, ya'll see, soon as ah can. Next year." But how could she with the other three, his older brother dead, shot to death in the street going to school? His brother had carried the stuff now and then to make money to give his mother and buy the new things he wanted. But he never would. Never, Sonny thought. His brother, the anger made his mouth taste sour.

He remembered after his brother died, when his mother stopped crying, she'd said, "Ah never want to say that boy's name in this house agin. Not ever agin."

"D'ya have any bike wheels?" he asked the angry-looking lady sitting behind the counter smoking a cigarette, letting it dangle like a weapon from her mouth. She motioned listlessly, like waving away flies, toward the back of the store. This was the only store, besides the grocery store, he'd ever gone into, so although most everything was broken, chipped, or ripped, his heart beat with excitement.

"Move yer bike outta the way, boy!" the woman yelled as someone knocked it over trying to get in. "Ah know, ah know," she muttered under her breath, "they steal yer teeth weren't in your goddamned mouth."

He ran to pick up his bike, and he looked at her, saying sorry, silently, with his eyes. Then he rolled it over to the far wall, listening to it creak and moan with age. There was just a patch or two of blue still left on the frame itself; the rest was rust and bare steel. He propped it up against the dark water-stained wall, patting it quickly like a friend.

He thought of his sister and brothers back at the apartment by themselves and how his mother would beat him with the belt if she got back before him. But she wouldn't. She never did. She'd be out past dinner. Maybe he'd even have to put them to bed, adding sweaters, if he could find them, to their clothes to keep them warm during the night. Dinner would be cold cereal, some bread, water from the tap. There was just enough milk for the cereal. Maybe the baby was putting something into the socket right now and getting killed. Maybe the older one had opened the door and they were wandering around outside looking for him, going into the street. Now the baby was being run over by a car.

Sonny sighed, his mouth dry with anxiety. He'd sat them in a group and threatened them with a beating, no dinner, no nothing, if they didn't stay put while he was gone. He'd given them one piece of bread with a little margarine on it, poured the remaining apple juice into three cups, filling it up with water the rest of the way. It hinted of apples, their sweetness. They'd had real apples a few times. They'd cut them into pieces, staring at the fleshy whiteness with curious eyes. Then he remembered the taste, which was better than candy.

Maybe she'll bring home some apples tonight, Sonny thought. "Only the damn dealer kin ford the damn apples from this damn store," his mother would say like a curse, passing by the over-priced, bright red apples side by side in their square wooden cribs. "Only the damn dealer gotta car ta go ta the market outta the damn neighborhood. Shit."

He'd gone there once with his older brother on the handlebars of his brand-new bike. He'd felt so proud riding on the handlebars, ahead of his brother. He'd smiled all the way. In the market his brother had bought milk, bread, eggs, even some meat, for his mother, things like that. Sonny had stood outside with the bike, his brother telling him, "Anyone try ta mess wich ya, donchya leave this bike, chill?"

Sonny had nodded wordlessly, watching his brother walk into the brightly lit store. He watched the doors open of their own accord with absolute wonder. There'd been a big, brown, plastic horse in front of the store. A child had ridden it while his mother stood by looking slightly impatient and bored. But first she'd put some money into it, which made it lurch with spastic joy as the child laughed high and sweet. After they'd gone into the store he'd walked over to the horse, rolling the bike alongside him, hearing it click-click-click like a new thing. He'd touched the horse, patting it, looking around to make sure no one was watching him. He'd looked up to the horse's brown plastic face and thought it was smiling at him. He saw that it had no teeth. No teeth. Nothing to bite with, making its face look so soft and inviting. He liked that horse more than anything he'd ever seen. He fingered the coin slot, circling it with his finger.

"Yer too old f'that shit. Wanna coke n some chips?" His brother had laughed, seeing Sonny fingering the coin slot with sheer longing. Sonny'd removed his finger with a burnt jerk and, standing nervously erect, quickly said, "Sure, Big Al."

He'd called his brother Big Al because everyone did, though he was small for his age. He was only twelve, but even the older guys on the street kind of respected him because he got his job done without a lot of explanations or being scared or acting confused about anything like younger boys do. He just did what he had to do, and then he waited for his money like a grown man. So they started calling him Big Al, though in fact, he looked no older than around ten.

Sonny picked out the two best tires in the bunch; he could see the others were even worse than what he had on his own bike. Every time he went out for a ride he expected to roll it home, the old bald tires finally punctured with all the broken glass he couldn't really avoid because it was everywhere, glittering with a quiet, self-satisfied menace. He hated broken glass. He hated his bald tires. He hated, he thought, almost everything: the dirty smell of the store, the old unwashed clothes, old sweaty shoes (he looked at his own where his big toe poked through the canvas and he hated his shoes and his toe); the unswept floors, for the first time, loomed out at him. The dirt and dust seemed (his ugly, naked toe) to be on everything, especially the broken, chipped, ripped up things (just like me, he felt with his familiar, diffuse sense of shame).

As he turned to leave, sweeping his eyes over the sprawl of sudden ugliness, which felt unbearable to him now, he clutched the two best tires in his left hand. His eyes rested for a moment on a strange sight: a small pile of seashells. He'd never been to the sea. He'd never heard it or touched it, so he wondered if they were fake. Sonny spread them flat with his right hand. "Chipped," he muttered. But there was shiny stuff on one of them like a rainbow. He picked it up, feeling its smoothness, trying to see if the rainbow felt cool or hot. It was just smooth like nothing. He'd heard of rainbows, and he'd seen pictures of some in school a couple of times in his reader. But he'd never seen a real one because he never really looked up and no one had ever said, "Hey, Sonny, git yer ass out here n take a look at this fuckin rainbow!" So he thought that rainbows were just another thing they told you about that you couldn't have. Another lie about nothing. Another thing you couldn't buy like the beautiful, white-fleshed, red apples. Or real meat. Milk. Enough of it. The list was endless, and he felt it like a terrible disease that was somehow his fault: poverty.

He switched the piece of shell to his left hand, closing it—he had no pockets without holes—and walked up to the counter. "How much're these?"

"Those be two-fifty, boy." The woman waited.

Sonny's hand closed tighter on the rainbow thing. "I only got two dollars."

"They be two-fifty." She looked away. For a split second she wanted to say, "Well, take em," but then a stronger voice said, "No one never gave you nothin." She lit another cigarette and listened to the boy's old bike roll past her with angry irritation.

"Shut that door!" He'd left the door wide open and now the wind blew in gusts, scattering paper in from the street. "Damn kid be a junkie next year," she hissed. Tears formed, involuntarily, at the corners of her eyes as she refused to name the faces of her own children, some gone, some dead. She refused to name them, but the awful warmth of a tear trailed her face so very slowly.

He no longer cared if they were dead or in the street or hungry, or even if his mother came home before him. He didn't care if anyone saw him up on the brown plastic horse as he put quarter after quarter inside the slot, letting the brown plastic thing take him far away, past everything he hated, past everything he could never have.

He didn't make a sound; no sound of joy for the long dreamed-of ride. Take me to Big Al, Sonny said in his mind to the brown plastic dead thing. The sharp edge of the rainbow shell cut into his hand, but he welcomed it as he thought of his brother.

He got off the dead thing and left his bike outside the store unprotected. He walked through the doors that opened, magically, of their own accord into the brightness of all the food in the world. There were so many apples, but he took only one large, bright red, white-fleshed apple. For a moment he wanted to steal another, but he saw them watching him. He knew the remaining change in his hand wasn't enough for two.

He would stop and talk to the men that promised him a new bike, and he would do whatever they said.

Birth of a Shell ❖

The day was hot and the ocean was so still it looked like a lake—a great, monstrous, light blue lake with small rows of lapping waves. It wasn't yet noon and the sand shimmered with spirals of heat. There were scattered beach umbrellas like bright, stiff Popsicles poking out of the littered, oil-stained sand. There were mainly women with their children; there were a few women alone, some men alone watching the women alone. The mothers, some of them, kept anxious eyes on their children. The ocean was never entirely trustworthy. A few of the mothers hadn't been to the shore since the summer before, and their journey by bus, dragged by hot, fitful children, seemed like a journey across the world. The lunch and a towel or two were in bags as the children ran around in the waves in their underwear. Where would they get money for bathing suits when underwear was hard enough? The cold beers food stamps wouldn't buy. A few of these women glanced away as the tide rolled a child under. They were tired, these women. Tired.

Lucinda was one of these women, but she watched the children with anxious eyes as they dared the ocean, screaming with high-pitched delight. She sketched them in her portable pad, adding color only at the end and sparingly. She was a painter. She hadn't painted for over two years, not since the children had been taken from her. She looked after and sketched these beautiful children, but they weren't hers. Hers were gone. Swept away as these screaming, beautiful children could be swept away by the untrustworthy sea.

Whenever Lucinda tried to sketch her own, her hand would tremble, lose its confidence, even with the current photos her ex-husband sent almost monthly. He, the dentist, paid torturer, sanctified giver-of-pain, culturally canonized god-of-the-teeth, had taken her children, calling her incompetent, unfit: crazy. Now the god-of-the-teeth sent her monthly photos of her son and daughter out-of-the-kindness-of-his-heart. When they'd come for them, the boy, the oldest, screamed MOMMY as they forced him from her arms. She'd frozen, watching them carry him, his eyes locked into hers in wide-eyed terror, as they carried him to the car. She hadn't seen them carry the baby, her daughter, right past her. Gone.

The god-of-the-teeth had left her their small beds, clothes, toys. No, he hadn't been totally ruthless; he took only their bodies. The bodies she'd felt grow and stretch and kick inside her own body. The bodies she'd known were hers as much as her own body. How would they do it, she wondered dully, as though she had to remember something as simple, as mundane as where food goes when the body craves it. Would they take my body, kicking and screaming, and leave my soul to fend for itself among the artifacts of my leftover, now-dead life. She smiled.

"Well, that's what he did, he killed me and all I have left are my hands, this pad, O god-of-the-teeth." She spoke to the sand quietly.

A man, who watched Lucinda, mistook her smile for an invitation and asked her name.

She looked at him without fear or rage or curiosity and said, "I don't know, what's yours?"

Hilda knew the end of the month would make her do it. How else could she do it? No money. No nothin. Pitiful scraps from food stamps to last the entire month for five children. How the hell they expect children to *live?* she asked in her mind, loudly. Louder than the soft hiss of water that touched her baby's feet. She felt her daughter's sweet baby body, and she knew what she should've done. Do those good Christian folks bring me milk and bread for my babies? Do they stand in line at the clinic with me and my babies? Do they make the state give funds for my backward child? I ain't seen them since they said, all smiling, You're doing the right thing.

Hilda pulled her daughter close and stood up, carrying her out to the curling waves. As the waves reached her thighs, cool and long they felt, she let the waves lap her waist and splash over her daughter's face, making her gasp for air and cry loudly.

Hilda turned back to the shore, watching the heat rise, curling from the sand. Her other children played without looking toward her. Soon they'd be hungry and all she'd brought was bread and butter, some lemon juice.

"Shoulda done it," she murmured.

Tomorrow night she'd take the kids over to her sister's and stay out all night till she had enough for the end of the month.

"Buy a ham, some pineapple slices." Hilda spoke to her baby and smiled. The baby smiled back.

The sun was so hot and it wasn't quite yet noon, and the children of the city without money played at the oily edges, and the children of the city with money left in their parents' cars to where the edge wasn't so oily.

After this was over she planned to go to Europe, France first. Paris. Lily's long, silky blonde hair was swept up, tied into a tight knot. Her huge tanned belly lay exposed to the hot sun. The child kicked and thrashed. It would be large, she could feel it. It was an it to her, not a boy or a girl. She imagined it faceless, though the father, like herself, was blonde. She didn't touch her belly, the it.

It wasn't hers. It was theirs. They paid her for it. Whatever it was. She smiled, remembering their choice: intercourse or insemination. The wife wanted to watch; either way she wanted to be there. "Do you want an orgasm? he'd asked after he'd deposited his sperm. "It might hinder conception," the wife protested as neutrally as possible. "But it might make a happier child if it takes," he answered as rationally as possible, still out of breath. "No, thank you," Lily had interrupted in a tone as polite and disinterested, as if a waiter had asked her if she wanted a second cup of coffee.

She sat up. It gave her no peace now on her back. "Three more weeks to go and I'm gone. Free." She gazed out to the horizon, but sky and sea just merged, making her restless, hungry. She brought out her healthy breeder's lunch, as she called it, and ate.

She picked up the paper and read an article about some right-to-lifers picketing an abortion clinic. "Sell it, stupid," she muttered to the unseen pregnant women the angry, sweating faces in the photograph wished to stop. Lily could read their obvious thoughts: They would save the unborn, the its, from these monstrous, unfeeling, godless women. Men and women with their angry, sweating faces. They sure don't look moral to me.

Lily laughed suddenly, thinking of the French Riviera and how she'd take off her top and expose her beautiful breasts to the sun. She oiled herself carefully, belly and breasts, to not ruin herself. And part of the agreement with the sweet couple was corrective surgery if any damage was done by it. Their it.

Lily stood up and saw the French Riviera, not the oily San Francisco beach with a bunch of screaming its. As she walked into the moving water, the child within her became still as the ocean filled her ears.

Sonia's hair was now dark red and her daughter's was now a soft auburn, and, just as their hair had changed, they had different names. At first her daughter had been confused. So she made a game of it: "Claire," she'd point and laugh as though it were very funny. "Claire is Mommy's girl. Claire goes bye-bye far, far away. Claire loves ice cream, doesn't she?" Sonia would ask, laughing. Then they'd eat ice cream and Claire became her name. Her new name.

She hadn't been two for very long when it happened; when Sonia had found blood on her daughter's diapers. Blood on their sheets. He'd stuffed them in the washer, too lazy to pour soap in and press a button.

No one believed her. Not even her parents. She always had a wild imagination, they'd said. Such a good man, she should be grateful. I never owned my own home, her mother told her. Why do you work? It happened because you work. Probably that woman's son . . .

Her daughter continued to bleed off and on, the rashes on her tiny labia, the sudden screams at night. Sonia would find her crouched in the corner of her crib because the Bad Thing was coming. The Bad Thing that wouldn't stop was coming. It was coming now.

Sonia was accepting a job in Japan. He'd never, ever find them now. Her nursing degree was in her maiden name. She'd use it, slightly modified, with a new first name. Sonia she'd chosen because she'd never really liked her given name, Mary. Mary, Mama's girl—Mary, Daddy's girl—Mary, Everybody's girl—Mary, the girl.

Sonia was a woman's name and one that she chose and she was grateful to no one because she'd given it to herself. And Claire: renaming her they'd left the terrified Cathy behind, always waiting for the Bad Thing.

On the plane, going to San Francisco, Claire lay sleepily in her arms and Sonia had said, "The Bad Thing, your daddy . . ." Cathy's eyes had widened at his name, naming the Bad Thing . . . "will never, ever, hurt you again because I won't let him." She'd held her daughter to the window and pointed to the clouds below. They were thick, spongy clouds and there were mean faces in them, but Cathy didn't cry because the Bad Thing was far, far away, under the mean faces in a place she used to know that made her scream.

Sonia watched Claire as she sat at the edge of the tide line and soft foamy fingers delighted and cooled her.

"Do you want to make a castle?" Sonia smiled, sitting next to her daughter, letting the water reach her feet and legs. Claire nodded yes and began to dig. Sonia filled the bucket again and again, creating a circle of high-domed walls of wet sand.

Claire walked to the towels and brought back her small plastic doll. She placed it in the center of the castle. Her eyes became grave as she stared at her doll, sitting absolutely still.

"Is she afraid of the dragon?" Sonia asked softly.

"The Bad Thing," Claire whispered.

For a moment Sonia's mind teetered helplessly with rage as she looked from Claire to the doll in the center of the circle. It had dark brown hair the way Claire used to. Then, without thinking, Sonia picked up her daughter's bright yellow sand shovel and began beating the ground around the castle.

"I'm killing the Bad Thing! I'm killing the Bad Thing and he'll never hurt the little girl again because he's dead! I'm killing him, Cathy!"

Claire reached into the circle, picking the doll up and putting it to her cheek: "The Bad Thing is killed, baby," she murmured. "The Bad Thing is killed 'cause Mommy killed him."

The tide covered the castle, forcefully, as it began its high tide journey back to the sand. Sonia grabbed Claire with a shriek of surprise and ran to the safety of their towels.

Lucinda laughed as the man mumbled his name, got to his feet, un-gracefully, and stumbled twice in his effort to get away from a woman who didn't know her name. She wished she'd kept silent. Maybe he would've exposed himself if she'd looked a little terrified and intimidated. Then, as was her custom, when the great jewel was exposed, she'd laugh in huge gusts till tears streaked her face.

"Lose some, win some," she muttered. Her eyes had become unbear-ably heavy and though she wasn't sleepy she'd closed them. When she opened them an hour later she was covered in sweat, and flies walked across her face. She sat up, slapping them away, and she almost stood up to go to the water but quickly changed her mind. The slight breeze that was blowing was enough, and she had no desire to be wet. I have to save all my strength, she told herself as she often did.

She began to sketch the smallest child at the water's edge. A boy. A black child with blonde, kinky hair. His eyes flashed, shockingly blue, in his dark face. He was undeniably beautiful. They'll make him pay for it, she thought, for being tan all year long while their own white, wormy bodies get cancer and wrinkled. "Crazy white people pay for a fuckin tan." She laughed but it was false, looking at the beautiful boy and knowing what was in store for him. She was dark skinned with light sea green eyes. She looked for his mother, for someone looking at him, but she couldn't pick her out.

Giving the blue to his eyes, Lucinda thought of her favorite mural, the one she'd designed and painted. The one with the big, strong, brown-skinned women walking away from the viewer toward the green fields and tasseling corn in the distance, toward a ritual only for women. Their children safely home with grandmothers in the country of their origins where they belonged. "In the country of the Goddess." Lucinda smiled. "Of La Llorona." She laughed a genuine laugh, forgetting her children.

"Maybe I've become La Llorona." A moment of clarity, clear, clear like white light, came to her. She stopped sketching and looked at her legs and ankles, dirty, her clothing, dirty and torn here and there. She felt her hair, which she kept constantly in braids, oily. Slowly, she undid her braids and her scalp relaxed. Her hair was dark and thick, past her shoulders. It was stiff and coiled, and as she ran her hands through it, it was as though she liberated snake upon coiling snake. They stuck out from her head as her hand coaxed them free, making her look wild and strangely beautiful.

Lucinda looked all around her, getting to her knees. She wondered why the beach never had whole shells, only fragments like the broken, oil-stained sand dollar she picked up and threw back to the hot sand. She tapped her pencil against the sketch and found the beautiful boy with her eyes. She wished she could ask him to come and sit with her to get his features, his expression, more clearly. I look like I'm crazy, and I don't even have a cracker to offer him, she reminded herself.

"La Llorona," Lucinda murmured, remembering her son's eyes, his expression as he'd screamed MOMMY over and over. She would've cried had she tears left, had her eyes remembered how to cry. That salty wetness her body made.

A huge, sun-filled wave gathered itself to spill and curl and spill—all energy, coolness, roar. Perhaps it brought shells. Perhaps not.

Lucinda watched as the immense wave overcame the screaming children. Their screams were of play, not terror. When the wave receded, pulling the children harshly, making them tumble and roll, she couldn't see the beautiful boy. She ran to the laughing children, looking for him.

"Goddess," she hissed, throwing herself into the cool, welcoming water. It was salty, harsh. Irrationally, she thought, This is how shells are born.

❖ The Burden

Today she'd do it. She'd put it off too many times. How many times had she come into her daughter's room to pack her things in boxes? How many times had she fled, slamming the bedroom door in tears?

No, today she'd do it. Today was the day. She couldn't imagine keeping it exactly the way she'd left it. The day she disappeared. No, she'd lose her mind. She almost had. But Carlos, her lover, had reached for her, held her, staying with her day and night for over a week. He'd held onto her when the wild, inhuman scream had possessed her, turning her into a scream. A scream. A scream she'd never, ever forget as long as she lived. She'd scratched Carlos's face, and he'd held her hands, but he'd refused to let her go. When her nine-year-old son had run into the room terrified, Carlos had said, "It's okay, Nick, I've got her. Go to your room. It's okay."

Tonight they were getting together to talk about him moving in, maybe getting married. Married, she thought. Nick'll like that. He likes Carlos a lot. So does María. María. So *did* María, she reminded herself sternly, but it didn't help. It didn't help the pain; it remained fresh and excruciating, making her dizzy. But she didn't run from the room or begin to cry.

She opened her daughter's drawers and picked up her favorite sweater. Immediately, she wanted to press it to her face, to smell it. To smell her daughter one more time. But she resisted, placing it folded into the box marked Goodwill. Each sweater, blouse, skirt, pants—she saw María in them. Standing in them, sitting in them, walking out the door in them. Living in them. Now the underwear drawer: her first grown-up bikini panties, the new unworn bras, two of them. And, of course, the new one she'd had on the day she left for school. They'd had an argument about lipstick again. "Everyone wears lipstick, Mom. I mean, everyone!"

"You can wear lip sheen but not lipstick, María. You're just too young. Who knows, maybe next year if you stop hassling me. I didn't wear lipstick till I was sixteen."

"At sixteen I'll be wearing lipstick and driving, Christ!"

"That's enough, María. You're going to be late for school and I'm going to be late for work. Do you have your dance stuff? You have practice today, right?" Then she gave María dinner instructions, reminding her to come right home after lessons and to remind Nick to start his homework. Meeting her daughter's steady gaze, she'd felt an overwhelming sense of tenderness. María always did put the casserole or roast in the oven or start the hamburger or heat up the leftovers. Sometimes María made dinner from scratch to surprise her, and Nick would do the dishes to see pleasure spread itself across their mother's face.

She scooped the underwear drawer into the box and closed it quickly. Involuntarily, she began, again, trying to remember exactly, what her daughter was wearing. It must've been new, we'd just gone shopping, she reminded herself for the millionth time. The only thing she could remember was María looking back at her, once, at the door, angrily. But her voice had been soft, compliant, "Okay, no problem."

"What if I said you can wear a subtle pink or coral next year?" She'd smiled. "I guess I don't want my little girl growing up too fast, m'hija. You're only thirteen, honey."

María had stopped and turned, facing her mother. She'd smiled widely, unselfconsciously, like a little girl. "Do you promise, Mom? For real, do you promise?"

"I promise, for real."

"I love you, Mom!" she'd shouted with a laugh and ran out the door, almost skipping.

She shut her eyes, but she still couldn't see María's outfit as she superimposed color, fabric, and pattern over her daughter's retreating girl/woman, girl/woman, girl/woman figure; the unmistakable body that had been her daughter, María, before she'd disappeared into the dark, thick hiding places of air and earth; at that very moment she'd turned into the scream. Into the scream. *Into the scream.*

Every instinct was screaming, Get in your car, look for her, look for her, look for her, how can you trust them to look for her the way you'd look for her, how can you trust them to ask the right questions, the right questions, how will they recognize her even if they find her, pictures are so unreliable, how will they know her eyes when they see her, her expression, her mouth, how it looks sad even when she's happy, how calm her mouth is, how calm her mouth is, how calm her mouth is, how her whole face comes together starting from the sides of her ears that stick out slightly when her hair's pushed back, how it follows her sweet, dark cheek that turns deep red with anger or joy, how the cheeks, the profile is unmistakably hers, how the whole face comes together when she speaks, and the mouth is not calm but restless, moving, moving, and the eyes are alive with light and shadow, and the face is unmistakably hers, my daughter's, María, my daughter's face, the one I've known since I first held her, how I protected her, how I protected her from harm, hunger, cold, boredom, harm, hunger, cold, boredom, strange dogs, harm, hunger, cold, then the strangers, never, never, ever, ever talk to strangers, never, ever, ever go into a stranger's car, never, ever, ever, how there are mostly good people, but there are the few bad ones and you must be very, very, very careful of all strangers, all strangers, because you never, ever, ever know, you never know, you never know, how the face, my daughter's unmistakable face, changed each year, each year, subtly, changing, how will they recognize her, *her face*, her changing face, how can I trust them to *know* . . . her . . . my . . . daughter . . . her . . . *know*

"They've got his license plate, Rita! Someone, a kid, had the presence of mind to get his license plate. They'll find them any minute, you'll see." Carlos's voice was excited with the news, but he forced a comforting tone to it. He could see the immense effort it was for her to hold still, to not go stark raving mad. He could feel it acutely. He held her shoulders with both hands, covering them with as much tenderness as he had. "The candles look nice, peaceful."

Their reflections danced in the dresser mirror, shadowing Rita's face. Grief made her face strangely beautiful. Grief lent her pleasing features a quality that reminds us of beauty. Carlos saw it and sighed. "Do you want some more wine. It's chilled, your favorite."

Rita looked up. "I forgot to tell you about the license plate, I'm sorry. They told me too, but that was over an hour ago." Her voice began to break. "I'll take that wine. Sorry I didn't mention the license plate . . ."

"It's okay, it's okay. I just called again. How about some food?"

"Just the wine, please." She heard him in the kitchen and she relaxed. She stared into the mirror and saw her mother's eyes and she remembered. María lit candles just like my mother. She looked at the shells María had collected on their occasional trips to the beach. They were placed in a beautiful order—some nestled together, some of the most striking María had placed alone. Some of her favorite crystals, in the shape of stars, small to large, hung from the ceiling and the candlelight shone through them. During the day, sunlight came through the windows, throwing rainbows in every direction. Often, at night, María would light the candles and, putting on her music, stare into the mirror. Once she'd murmured to Rita, meeting her mother's eyes in the soft, glowing mirror, "I'm going to be a famous dancer someday, Mom." Her mouth had been calm with that glimpse of her future. So calm.

Rita picked up the wine and sipped it. "Anything," Rita murmured. "Anything can happen." Then she picked up a spiralling, white shell, worn from the tide—very, very white like bone. The tip came to a sharp, conical point. She pressed it into the palm of her hand. She would sit here and stay awake until they brought María home. But will they know her, will they recognize her, will they. . . . I will, she answered herself. I'll know her. I always have and I always will. Rita looked into the mirror and saw her mother's eyes, María's eyes. She passed her hand over the candle's flame and it briefly burned her. She pressed the seashell into the palm of her hand and it hurt, digging its point into her, keeping her awake, alive, quiet. Sane.

"I know you, María, don't be afraid, I know you, María, I know you, I know you, I know you, don't be afraid, don't be afraid, María," she chanted quietly over and over. Over the burning candles and María's carefully placed shells.

Almost everything was packed. Carlos would take the boxes to the Goodwill tomorrow. She couldn't bear to have a stranger pick them up. But someone should have them, some little girl/woman, woman/girl, girl/woman. He'd dragged her right off the street as she was walking with a friend and no one stopped him, no one, no one. He'd abandoned the car, blood in it, her left hand. He'd severed her left hand, leaving it like a trophy. Or was the trophy what he'd kept? she asked herself dully. They hadn't found María's body. Her girl/woman, woman/girl, girl/woman body. *Her body.*

Rage and a hate beyond the human, its now familiar, terrible comfort held her. All night she'd sat facing the candles in the mirror, facing María's carefully arranged shells, feeling her daughter's agony, pressing the white shell into her left hand to keep herself awake, alive, quiet. Sane. Then, suddenly, she'd felt a searing pain in her wrist, her left wrist, air being held from her lungs, hands on her own throat, the strange relief, the strange welcome relief after the terror, the agony all night. Then nothing. She felt nothing from her daughter. The agony stopped.

Standing, she began to scream, mouth open, howling without human consciousness. She could see María, her shadow, a soft white light being sucked out of her body—no, she was escaping her body, and someone, someone was holding her as she screamed, as she became nothing, a shadow, a soft white light, as her daughter filled her, so briefly.

Everything was packed. Even the curtains were off the windows. A relative would take the bed for her daughter. The hanging crystals were taken down, so the hot afternoon sun streaming through the windows created no rainbows. The room looked forsaken, naked. It was as though María's voice had never spoken in this room, as though her body had never filled the room with its presence and scent. As though her inviolate dreams had never taken shape within the shelter of this forsaken, naked room. The walls were indifferent, silent. No one spoke María's name. No one.

Rita stood facing the mirrored dresser and saw that she wasn't crying. She saw that her face had its mask of inhuman rage (unfulfilled certainty), hate (fulfilled certainty): endurance. To feel sorrow, love, now would kill her, destroy her; she had to endure.

She picked up a small cardboard box and swept the shells into it. Then she reached in, taking the white-as-bone, sharp-tipped shell and placed it in her shirt pocket. She placed a snug-fitting lid on the shells, and, shaking the box, they sounded like scattered, loose bones. A sad sound. Then she realized they'd probably throw the useless shells away, but she couldn't do it. She couldn't throw María's shells away. She added it to the mound of clothing, hiding it under the jean jacket, the one María had been so proud of because she'd found it at a secondhand store for a few dollars. So now it'd be third hand, fourth hand, hand upon hand.

All he'd left her was María's left hand, and even that had been disposed of after they studied it. She'd only heard of it. She'd never seen it, touched it, kissed it goodbye.

The hot afternoon sun poured through the windows, and without the curtains it was becoming unbearably hot. No rainbows danced on the walls; María's crystals were packed away with her new woman's underwear. Reaching down under the jean jacket, in spite of her desire not to, Rita picked up the box of shells. The sad bone sound echoed loudly in the hot, forsaken room. "Useless," she murmured. "Absolutely useless." She shook them again and again, listening to their sad rattling sound, like bones, and it soothed her. Strangely, it soothed her. She shook the box steadily as sweat began to pour down her face and her face began to soften. It began to soften with sorrow and love. Sorrow (unfulfilled longing) and love (fulfilled longing) merged in her depths like an exquisite orgasm. Tears streamed down her face softening her further.

She saw María in the doorway as she turned and smiled. She saw her clothing even to the color of her purple leggings. She would always be her little girl. She would never wear lipstick.

Then María laughed and said, "Do you promise, Mom?"

"I promise," Rita whispered. For the rest of her life she would wake and wish him dead, and if dead, unborn. Her therapist urged her to forgive him as a victim of his own sickness and go on with her life. To unburden herself. Yes, I'll go on with my life, she told herself. I'll marry Carlos. He's a good man and I love him, but I want this burden.

"María."

Rita continued to shake the scattered, loose bones in a steady rhythm. Maybe we'll have a daughter. I'm still young enough. The sound of the shells filled the room and the room stirred imperceptibly with life. She'll wear lipstick and become a mother and a grandmother and be with me as I die.

"I promise you, María."

María laughed, raising both hands in the air in a gesture of joy, holding them up, for a moment, like two hard-won trophies. "For real, Mom?"

Rita smiled at the empty room, imagining a crib with a pink comforter, pink curtains on the windows. The small dresses. "De verdad, hija. De verdad."

Rita looked into the mirror and saw her mother's eyes and her grandmother's eyes. María's eyes. She watched her left hand move, rhythmically. She sensed it, but she couldn't say it. The sound of the scattered, loose bones, sad and awkward in itself, called on its limitations, nothingness, death itself, to engage, make music out of sound and silence—to make new life out of the lost, scattered bones of her daughter. It existed between the sound and the silence, between the hand and the body, between hate and love. Between burden and blessing.

"I will know you, I will know you, I will know you, I will know you," Rita chanted, looking into her own eyes, hearing the bones of her daughter gathering life, slowly, so slowly, between earth and air.

"María."

The Edge of Darkness ❖

"Don't make a sound and just start driving and you'll live." He smiled as he held the gun low, close to his stomach, pointed at her.

There were people all around. She'd just paid for her gas and the gas attendant was talking to someone with his back to her. She wanted to scream, but she looked at the gun, and she saw how steady he held it. He smiled wider. He must be crazy, she thought.

"Take my purse. There's about fifty in it."

"I don't want your fuckin money," he laughed out loud. "I said drive, you stupid bitch."

"What do you want?" She forced herself not to cry.

He stopped smiling and stared into her eyes intensely. His eyes were very blue. "I want you." His voice was almost passionate.

"But what do you want?" She could only whisper. She knew if she spoke she'd scream.

"Start driving and you'll live." He smiled as though amused.

She turned the key, dreading the sound of the motor for the first time in her life. How many times had it refused to start? How many times had she called a neighbor to jump start her? How many times had she called Alice to pick her up on the way to work? How many times? she screamed, silently, to the old car as it came to life, and she pulled out of the gas station. Her hands were trembling violently, so she clutched the steering wheel till they hurt.

"Where should I go?" Tears choked her as they ran freely down her face.

"North till I say stop." He stopped smiling and stared at her as though he owned her completely. She belonged to him now. He rested the gun on his thigh, keeping it pointed at the center of her body. Occasionally, he glanced past her at the never-ending ocean. To the horizon that always made him feel so lonely.

It would be time to dance soon. She could hear the drums. Everything was prepared. Her ceremonial clothing fit her perfectly. Her thick, dark hair had been braided. She picked up the round, smooth abalone earrings made by her mother. They were light in color like the morning. When she looked at them, she could almost smell the ocean and hear its thunder and feel its spray. As she put them through her ears, she missed her mother freshly, as though she'd just died; and, again, she realized her mother would not see her dance as a woman today. But her Spirit will, she reminded herself. Remember, she promised she'd return for my first dance as a woman and the birth of my first child.

Something strange and unfamiliar bothered her, but soon she'd forget it entirely. As soon as she'd begin to dance, it'd be gone from her mind. The runner had reported that weak, ghostly men travelled, visiting with the inland clans. They weren't to be trusted—or killed, since they did nothing to provoke the People. They were too ghostly to be trusted. Their skin wasn't good and brown and strong like the People's. They were more pale than a newborn, and weak, and their language, if it could be called that, was ugly to hear. The inland People said their language was not beautiful.

She turned her head quickly to feel the earrings sweep the softness of her neck. Then she did it rhythmically as though she were dancing. She picked up the large, dark blue abalone, shaped like the moon and sun, that was threaded with feathers. She ran her fingers over the soft, white egret feathers that dangled from the strips of leather. One hawk feather, taken from the tail, was placed between the white ones. She counted the dark bands out loud with pleasure. Then she tied the abalone high on her braid, feeling the softness of feathers on her right cheek.

She picked up the other one, dangling it in front of her in the semidarkness. She smiled at the strange, surging joy that sang inside of her. In her womb.

She regained her composure. At least she wasn't crying anymore. They'd been driving for half an hour, heading north. Soon they'd be in Mendocino County. She thought of her two children with her mother, briefly; but she stopped herself because she couldn't stand the thought of not seeing them again. She thought of her husband and his black and hard, but kind, eyes. She imagined her mother calling him soon, wondering where she was. She imagined her husband's face wrinkling in confusion. She was never late. He'll know, she thought. He'll know and call the police. Maybe if I keep him out on the road they'll catch us. Yes, yes, that's it. It's the only way. She pushed her terror deep down, deep into her womb.

She glanced at him. He was in his late twenties, blonde, a little dirty, but not badly dressed. He'd said nothing since they started. She took a deep breath. "If you want the car you can have it, you know. With the money in my purse you could make it to Washington maybe." She made her voice sound reassuring.

He looked at her and the late afternoon sun shone into his eyes, but he didn't blink. They were transparent like the ocean on a clear, warm day, but cruelty played in them, making their transparency two terrible mirrors. He raised the gun, pointing it at her. He enjoyed gauging her fear. She's getting used to it, he thought, and he smiled. He let the gun rest again on his thigh.

"You some kinda Indian?" His voice held laughter.

"My people were Coastal Indians," she answered in the reassuring tone. "Now there's not many of us, even among the mixed bloods."

"Thought you were. So, I gotta squaw, huh?" He wondered what Indian women were like. I've had Black, Japanese, some brown meat, but not a Coastal Indian. He laughed out loud.

Anger rose to her throat, and she felt her face burn, but she made herself not grip the steering wheel and give herself away. "Are you from this area?" The sun would be setting in an hour or so. The kids are probably being fed now, she thought without meaning to. Her heart picked up speed, echoing loudly in her ears.

"Wouldn't you like to know." His voice was intimate and sinister. He had nothing to lose: no family, no friends, no nothing. Maybe I will go up to Washington after I'm through with Running Deer here. He smiled widely at his sudden decision and her new name.

"So's your name Running Deer? Did I guess it or what?"

When he finished laughing, she replied, "No, it's not."

"Well, what the fuck is it? You can tell me. We're goin to be good friends, you and me." Now he laughed softly.

Her first impulse was to lie, but she thought of her driver's license in her purse, so she said in the reassuring tone, "Lila."

"Don't give me that Lila shit, what's your squaw name?"

She glanced out at the reddening sky and saw a large female hawk on a power line. "Swift Hawk," she lied.

"No shit."

She repeated, "Swift Hawk," in a murmur and smiled, inwardly, to herself.

She placed the abalone with the egret and hawk feathers high on her left braid. She placed the rainbow-catching abalone choker around her neck. It pressed itself at the base of her throat, reminding her to be silent.

The drums grew louder, calling the women out to dance. The men's voices were high and full of longing and power. She knew he would be waiting to watch her dance. Soon they'd be woman and man together, and she'd dreamt her first child with him. A girl.

He'd called her his Sacred White Shell Woman when he'd held her close–and she had felt like her, for a moment, in his arms. A long, wonderful moment. She smiled, remembering.

"All is good, all is good," she murmured to the small fire at her feet. She picked up a sprig of sage and lit it, twirling it around her head and body. Then she pointed the sweet, smoking sage to the four directions, starting in the North and ending in the North. She prayed for guidance, beauty, harmony, strength.

"Give me many living children, Northern Mother. Make me wise." Then she giggled because she was still partially a child.

The older women entered silently. One of the women glanced at her with a hint of a smile. The oldest woman, the Grandmother, looked utterly stern and unyielding. She came forward and slapped her once, a stinging blow to her right cheek. To her embarrassment she began to cry.

"Good, that is good, young woman. May your tears be sweet and full of a woman's wisdom. May your children live. May the People live. Today you are sacred as White Shell Woman. Guard her well."

The women surrounded her and pushed her into the harsh sunlight. She'd been inside for four long days. They'd brought her small amounts of food and water and carried her waste away.

She joined the other young women, three of them. She closed her eyes and lifted her face to the sun and let the men's voices fill her heart. She began to hum deep in her throat. She could feel his eyes on her. She could see his face, clearly, as though her eyes were open. She saw his small abalone earrings shining like mirrors in the sun; but she didn't look. Today she belonged to no one. Not even to herself.

❖

"Okay, Swift Hawk, pull into this place," he said, indicating a motel to the side of the road. "Park it in front of number six."

There was no one to be seen. No one. The sun had set. Every inch of the road she'd waited for the sound of a siren to gain on them, but nothing. Her mouth went dry with terror.

"If we stop here you'll lose time going north, won't you?" She pitched her voice low, concealing the terror poised to leap screaming through her teeth.

"Listen, squaw, I got two more nights in this place, so we'll use it up and keep going after we get ta be good friends. Think we will go up to Seattle and get some construction work. Who knows, maybe put you to work hustling your sweet, little Coastal Indian ass." He laughed, seeing her shock. Now she'll be about right, he thought, lifting the gun. He put it to her head, feeling it hit her skull, and he heard her breath escape in a muted scream.

"Make any false moves, any noise, squaw, and I'll blow your head right off your fuckin shoulders, you got it?" He smiled in the darkness. He could feel her terror acutely, and it excited him as nothing else. Yeah, she's about right, he thought. Perfect, just perfect.

The drums and singing, the sun's warmth and light, fused and held her as she danced. In her right hand she carried a fan of dark cormorant feathers that caught the light into rainbows. She concentrated on this as she moved through the air. She was flying—flying over the earth and sea. She hummed deep in her throat, but she didn't sing. She touched the shell at her throat.

Her hunger and thirst were gone. For the first time in her life they'd left her without being satisfied. During the four days she'd thought about food and him, him and food, but now the cravings were gone as she flew straight toward the sun where all life begins. She was without fear, yet fear guided her way.

Now she would learn about the loneliness and fullness of creation.

She sat on the edge of the bed, naked and cold, though the room was warm. She shivered uncontrollably and kept her head down.

He was still dressed, having removed only his jacket. He picked up a small, white moon shell from the night table. There were eight of them. "Hey, didn't you Indians buy things with shells?"

She couldn't answer him. Her voice was gone. One arm was over her breasts, the other over her squeezed-together thighs.

He grabbed her arms, forcing them to her sides. He laughed harshly at the shame on her face. "I asked you a question, squaw. Speak up or I'll get rid of you right now. Be a good squaw, and I'll let you go in Washington. Maybe. So what about these shells, they like money?"

"They used to be," she whispered.

"Well, this one's to suck me off." He unzipped his jeans, bringing his swollen penis out, carefully, between the zippered teeth. He moved toward her and shoved the beautiful, white moon shell between her legs as he thrust into her mouth toward the back of her throat. She cried out, involuntarily, gagging her lunch and choking.

He stopped and slapped her hard, making her head swing back. "Not a sound, bitch! Not a fuckin sound, do you hear me?" Then he smiled as though they'd reached an understanding. "Only seven more shells to go, Swift Hawk. You ever do this before?"

She shook her head, no.

"Answer me, bitch!"

"No." Tears ran down her face.

"You can cry. Yeah, that's okay."

She sat in the Full Moon light, coming to herself in the silence. Soon she'd eat a hot stew, some tea, some sweet berries. The moon's light was harsh and bright on the stones surrounding her, but it was a bright, gentle path on the swelling sea. The sea sang to her of patience, pain, and pleasure. The sea sang to her a Woman's Song, and it was as though she'd heard it all her life, but for the first time she understood the words. She touched the dark blue disc at her throat.

She accepted the moon's light on her woman's body. She accepted the cycles of creation. Sun and Moon she was. "Sun and Moon," she murmured. A great wave of hunger embraced her, and she laughed out loud.

She wanted to go and eat, but she couldn't just yet. It was too beautiful.
When I'm a grandmother, she thought, I'll remember this night. How I love the
edge of darkness.

❖

She lay dazed as he went to the bathroom. Her throat and mouth were
sick from his semen and her vagina and anus were ripped and raw. She
thought she'd vomit again but it stopped at the back of her throat at the
thought of the beating he'd given her when she'd vomited, splattering him
with it. She touched her anus, gently, and she whimpered seeing the bright
blood on her fingers.

Four shells to go, she thought with the part of her mind that believed
him; but the part of her mind that didn't said, Then he'll start all over
again. And she knew it was true. And it was unbearable. Utterly unbearable. Unbearable.

She saw her purse on the floor and reached for it though her bones
ached from his beatings. The knife, she thought, the knife must be here.
She moved the objects in her purse silently, though she was terrified he'd
return too soon. This time he'll kill me, she thought with sudden clarity.
He'll use up all the shells in the sea, the thought came to her and, for a
moment, she glimpsed a woman covered in white shells. Her face was
stern. Unyielding.

Her hand closed on the switchblade she'd carried as a girl to go fishing.
She'd been swift and thorough cleaning her catch. She'd cleaned her
younger brother's catch as well. Many times they'd eaten from the sea.
She was a good fisherwoman, and she could kill and gut a fish in minutes.

She opened the blade, holding it under her right leg, flat and cold against
her skin. She breathed deeply a few times, trying to calm her mind. If she
missed, she knew, she'd have no more chances. "He'll use up all the shells
in the sea," she murmured, and she remembered the face of the White
Shell Woman: unyielding.

"What're you talkin to yerself, Swift Hawk?" he said, laughing as he approached the bed. "Maybe we should call room service and change the
sheets. Pretty goddamn bloody and you had to go and barf on everything,
you stupid bitch." He threw her his used towel. "Here, wipe that shit off."
He watched her with a vague interest. She isn't terrified anymore, he realized. Fucking bitch's giving up on me. He took a drag of his cigarette, ex-
haling with impatience.

She reached for it, slowly, with her left hand and wiped her neck and belly. She refused to wipe her vagina in front of him. She moved listlessly, waiting, waiting, holding the sweet, sharp knife under her body.

"Well, are you ready for shell number five, Swift Hawk? Shit, maybe a couple of cigarette burns'll turn you on." His shirt and pants were off, but he kept his shorts on.

Anger flashed across her eyes, but she held still, remembering to breathe. She clutched her knife firmly, calmly, in her right hand.

He jumped across her, pinning her down, laughing. "Hey, that's better, you're pissed off again. I thought you and I had s'more t'go, Swift Hawk. Four more shells and all." He slapped her with the back of his hand and her nose began to bleed. Straddling her, he removed his penis from his shorts. The sight of her bleeding nose excited him and her eyes were full of defiance.

"Here, suck this till it's hard. Wait, I forgot the fuckin shell." He reached over for it and the knife went into his soft, white belly. She ripped upward, gutting this huge, horrible fish. She saw the large hawk in her mind's eye as she spread her wings to swoop.

"Hey!" he shouted in surprise as she pushed him away from her. Then he lay on his back staring up at the ceiling. She slit his throat, feeling the warmth of his blood on her hands and his blood smelled thick and sweet. She lifted her left hand and tasted his blood. It was salty. Like the sea.

As she drove south she was glad she'd filled the tank. Her face was cut and bleeding though she'd showered before she left. Pieces of toilet paper clung to her face, catching the blood and drying it. Some of them soaked through, and she replaced them with the roll beside her. She'd folded a wash cloth and placed it between her legs to catch the blood that still came. More slowly now.

Her eyes threatened to close from exhaustion, but she made herself open them wider. She pulled over to the side of the highway, opening the window that faced the sea. She opened her purse and removed something small wrapped in bloody newspaper. She threw it toward the sea, saying, "This is a gift from Swift Hawk, sacred Mother. Mother of all life. Mother of all death. Sacred, oh my sacred, White Shell Woman, this dick is for you." The strength in her voice surprised her, and she didn't weep. Instead, a strange peace flooded her.

"When I'm a grandmother," the words came to her, "I'll always remember this night."

The enormous full moon was setting, a deep blood red, at the edge of darkness.

✤ Merman

Liz hoped no one would sit next to her. After all the readings, the work-shops, her talks, the only thing she longed for was to sit in silence and stare at clouds and glimpses of Earth. The plane hummed beneath and all around her. It felt utterly luxurious to sit, without even a poem poking at her consciousness. Though the event of taking off from the ground, leaving the Earth for a bit—the defiance of gravity—almost always produced one, a poem, of its own accord.

Words, Liz thought with her usual mixture of gratitude and resignation—without words, no meaning. The plane means nothing to me—it becomes only transportation—without the ritual of words and the words that came before. *The words that create me.* In her poetry this realization was evident, but, later, in her talks she avoided such direct, metaphysical statements. She'd come to realize that to be too blatantly spiritual was to be considered feebleminded, but to be appropriately sly was to be smart, zen-like. Intelligent.

Liz was forty-six. She'd won her share of awards, but she knew that there was nothing as unattractive as an aging woman with runaway spiritual hormones. First it's the sexual ones, now this. She smiled at her invisible audience. The words that create you, but her topic had been form and content. She was good. She slipped out of their headlocks and spoke about a line as though the universe depended on it. She loved her lack of punctuation.

When he sat down next to her she refused to look and acknowledge him. She kept her eyes closed, attempting to convey her level of tiredness, exhaustion, disinterest. The plane began to roll, picking up to takeoff speed. Then the unbelievable lift. She opened her eyes to watch the world disappear.

"That's my favorite part." His voice was young and full of undisguised energy. There was an unexpected poise to his words that made her look at him.

She was stunned. He wasn't handsome—he was beautiful. His beauty was of a kind of integration, a wholeness, a mesmerizing combination of black hair, clear green eyes, flawless cream-colored skin, and grace. His face was entirely at peace and confident, and though his eyes automatically ex-tracted approval, there was no hint of arrogance in them. He wore thin gold chains around his neck and a large gold chain bracelet on his tapered wrist. Not that he was delicate—he wasn't. He looked to be at least six feet, but in a kind of perfect proportion and utterly at ease with himself.

If I were twenty, Liz thought, I'd probably faint, but I'm old enough to be his mother. Then she couldn't help adding, Hope I don't look too far over the hill. She shrugged inwardly and smiled at him.

"Are you going to San Francisco?" the beautiful voice asked.

"I live there. Where're you from?" Liz looked at him in a direct, friendly manner, refusing to succumb to the surprising feminine response that was making her blush. She'd never seen such perfect male beauty. She re-peated like a mantra, I'm forty-six, I'm forty-six, I'm forty-six. . . .

"I'm visiting from South Africa." He smiled at her. There didn't appear to be one unselfconfident bone in his body. He had the bearing of a fu-ture king. The world was made for him. It belonged to him, and he was universally loved.

A chill went up her spine. "Did you say South Africa?" Now she tried to hide instant revulsion, knowing it would close communication.

"Yes." He smiled openly, revealing perfect, the most perfect teeth she'd ever seen. Absolutely white, without blemish. "Would you like anything?" he indicated the stewardess with the drink cart.

"I'll take some white wine." The stewardess reached over, handing her a bottle and a cup. The look on her face was of sheer envy. He's mine, he's mine, her eyes couldn't help saying.

"Jesus," Liz murmured. This guy's a walking snare, she thought, pouring her wine. He should be outlawed.

The stewardess poured his drink possessively. She glared at Liz and left, clanging her bottles.

There was a black couple right across from them and in front of them a black woman with her child. The child peered over her seat, already getting restless with hours to go. "I'm thirsty," she whined. "You just wait," her mother told her. The black couple laughed at something, then kissed.

Liz looked at the beautiful prince from South Africa to see if he noticed the couple. His eyes were straight ahead, at peace, clear and shining. Absolutely at peace. Liz sipped the chilled Chablis and, crossing her left leg over her right leg, angled her body, subtly, in his direction.

"What brings you here to the United States?" When he turned his full attention on her it was hard not to feel like the fainting twenty-year-old. Forty-six, she told herself, and never seen anything like this. Goddess, Goddess.

"Oh," he smiled widely again, "it's probably my last chance to see everything. I'm on a worldwide tour for a year before I start work with my father."

His teeth were like neat little seashells all in a row and his eyes were like the sea. Not just green, but *green*. Her muse stirred. Her muse shouted, A merman. . . .

"How do you like it here?"

"A fascinating country. So vast. So diverse and quite beautiful." He raised his drink, and his gold bracelet slid, gracefully, up his forearm and back down to his wrist.

She took the plunge. "Is it hard to be mingling freely with black people like we do in the United States?" Her voice was pitched with caution.

"Why, no." He looked genuinely startled. A shadow briefly crossed his beautiful face, but the wide seashell smile swallowed it, whole. "They have their rights here. I studied your country, you know." His eyes widened. "Oh, look, look at those clouds. It makes you want to walk on them!"

"Well, I hope you'll forgive me if I probe a little, but I've studied your country, too, and I'm curious."

"Quite all right." His smile was luxurious. It was innocent.

"Well, I'm curious, do you know any black people at home?"

"Why, yes, they work with us. They are people like us."

"Liz was astounded. "Really, do you mean you have black friends?" Maybe his family's one of the few radicals.

"Why, certainly, yes." The smile, the smile, the sea green merman eyes. The flawless, cream-colored skin.

"So, you go out to dinner, visit each other's homes, stuff like that?" His face registered distaste, and she thought her choice of the word "stuff" had offended him, not a precise word. Ill-used.

"What I mean is, you actually have friendships with black people, go out and enjoy each other's company? I thought, everything I've heard or read has been to the contrary. Is that difficult for you, socially?"

His face was averted as he stared at his drink, but his hands looked relaxed, poised. Then he looked at her with an exquisitely controlled exasperation, a genuine sense of shock, as though he had to explain the process of breathing. "That," he paused. "That would be impossible." He paused again. "To be seen together would be impossible." He paled visibly.

It was unthinkable. This woman's unthinkable. Perhaps hysterical, his brain responded with a jolt. Everything I know. . . . It was as though she'd suggested his most feared horror. Perversion, the feeling, but not the word, hovered in his consciousness.

"Then how can you call them friends?"

"They work with us, and I know them. We wouldn't have it any other way, you know." The smile was faded, the luxuriant ocean had receded, but he was still beautiful though momentarily disturbed at her words, the perversion; dry land claimed him. But it was only momentary. Soon it would rectify itself and the world would go on as it should, "We wouldn't have it any other way. . . .

. . . you know." Liz could feel him readying himself for the deep, cool dive. Escape. She threw out her hook, "What if. . . ." She let her words pause and gather. Didn't she, the poet, know the power of words? Wasn't she forty-six? Shouldn't she say it? "What if you were born black? What if your skin," she pinched her own skin and looked at him, holding his eyes, "was black, not white?"

There was one of the workers, a black who'd worked for over three years with his father's business. He'd saved enough money to go home for a visit, to see his wife and sons. He'd come to him, shy, apologetic. Well, don't I speak on familiar terms to the blacks? Don't I? And this black was quiet, efficient, especially contained. He never noticed their features—their faces were so black—but this one had a scar on his left cheek and his manner was admirable, almost intelligent.

One of his sons had requested a seashell. They were far inland and his father worked by the coast. But how? How would he get a seashell?

When he'd brought it to him, tears had gathered at the corners of the black's eyes. It had fit in the palm. When he'd handed it to him their skins had touched, briefly. He remembered it, clearly, now, with this woman, this horrible woman, pinching her skin, "*not white?*"

A Beautiful, Haphazard Design ✣

He was nervous as he rang the bell. They'd talked on the phone last night, and they'd laughed like old friends a few times, but it'd been nearly six years since they'd seen each other. Their son, Felipe, had travelled back and forth by plane between California and Texas since he was twelve. Now, Felipe was in college and saw both of them, his parents, on semester breaks, but he was really closer to his mother.

Leo rang the bell again, a little longer, and wiped off the sweat that kept gathering on his upper lip. His face was fairly smooth; he thanked his Indian blood for that. Though when he was a teenager he'd wanted a mustache like some of his friends. His had grown out thin and scraggly, and his friends had nicknamed him Fu Man Chu, so he shaved it off. He pressed the bell long and hard for the third time and finally heard her voice, "Hold your horses!"

The basket of seashells, shiny and perfect, wrapped in cellophane, looked suddenly awkward and adolescent. So did the bottle of champagne he held in his other hand. As he heard her steps rushing to the door, he had to restrain himself from throwing them both down the hall in a last-ditch effort not to appear overanxious and ridiculous. In fact, Leo still didn't know why he'd called her to talk and then suggested they go to dinner. He grasped at a convenient excuse, the most obvious, that streaked by just before Ramona opened the door: I'm in Los Angeles and she's in San Francisco, so why not?

"Speak of the devil!" Ramona began to laugh unselfconsciously as though he were an old friend she hadn't seen for years. Her eyes held the old mischief.

"Yeah, it's me, Ramona. You look damned good. This fast northern gringo life seems to agree with you. You look good, girl." Leo smiled like a little boy. This was his charm and he knew it.

"Ay Dios, the same old tricks too. ¡Qué cabrón!" Ramona rolled her eyes upward in mock despair. Then she rolled them down again, staring directly into his. "You're looking pretty good yourself. Staying in shape, I see, in good old El Paso, macho, Lone Star State, et al."

"You aren't going to start, are you?" His eyes glittered.

"Of course, I am. I'm a lawyer, remember?" She smiled slyly like a cat. Her body remembered his with a shiver. His masculinity.

"I remember. We never did resolve who was the better one, did we?" Leo dropped his gaze to the seashells. He was suddenly glad that he probably looked awkward standing there in the doorway with gifts. Gifts for her. "This is for you. And so is this."

Ramona took the basket of shells and champagne with a nod of her head, a silent gesture of thanks and stood aside making room for Leo to enter. She walked quickly to the kitchen. "Shall I open this or what?"

"Sounds good to me." Leo surveyed the front room, in a sweep, with pleasure. She always made a beautiful home, he thought. Felipe's photo was on the mantle over the fireplace. A small, warm fire burned, offsetting the cold fog outside. He looked into Felipe's strong, brown, handsome face and, again, he couldn't really say who he resembled most, Ramona or himself. Next to Felipe's photo was a small spray of orchids. Leo bent forward to smell them, but found no scent.

"Felipe's getting ready for finals. He called yesterday. Has a new girlfriend named Honey. Imagine? I couldn't stop laughing. It seems she's from India, and her parents are rich or something." Ramona handed a full glass of the Spanish champagne to Leo and looked at his hips, briefly, approving of them as she had long ago when she met him. She'd always liked his hips. Men's hips, chests, shoulders, the long muscled thighs. Men's bodies. She licked her lips, tasting old memories and laughed at herself, silently.

"Does she wear a sari and all?"

"I forgot to ask. Well, a toast?"

Leo had seen her glance at his hips. He smiled, inwardly, at her old sexual aggression and realized, with a jolt, how sexy she was. There was something about the way she stood that said, I like sex. She didn't look forty-four. He wondered if he looked forty-seven. "To Eros in the second half of life," Leo said, sighing. Then he laughed, a little too loudly.

Ramona looked at him knowingly. She'd stopped seeing him, just talking to him on the phone, because of this. First the violent lovemaking, then the violent conflict. Who was boss? Who was the aggressor? Who was the alpha wolf? Looking at him, calmly, after the years of separation, she realized she still loved him, but she wasn't in love with him. That hot fire, that torture he could always dangle her over when his will, his command, failed him.

Ramona stepped back from Leo and sat on the couch, her favorite spot. My couch, she thought, patting it reassuringly. What's the difference between loving and being in love? And then she realized, with a shock of clarity, that to love was not to be in someone's power, and to be in love was to be in someone's power. She turned it over in her mind as she gazed at the shiny shells in the basket, but she still didn't quite understand. Why? Ramona asked herself as she picked up the basket full of shells.

"Well, are you in love with someone, speaking of Eros?" She smiled, but her eyes were without humor. "They must've polished these to make them look so perfect," Ramona murmured to herself.

"I guess you know from Felipe I'm not living with Cathy anymore. So, no, I'm not in love with anyone. Maybe in lust here and there. How about you?" Leo gulped his champagne down at once, feeling the tiny bubbles burn his throat.

She looked at him, and it was as though they were still together, though she could feel the presence of the women he'd been with last. But she liked it. It made him strange. Exciting. Not hers.

"I'm seeing someone special, I guess. But I don't think we're in love. Yet. We seem to be getting closer and closer, but it's as though we both want to make sure this is the real cosa, you know?" Ramona smiled. "Balanced passion, I guess."

"You've lost your Tex-Mex accent completely living up here. You sound like a true grin-ga," Leo smiled back. "Well, I suppose you can wait forever to make sure it's the co-sa, but it sounds like you're wiser or something."

"A grin-ga, huh? Well, I can still spik flewent the espanish, ya know. Chev a lay and al that shit, pues," Ramona laughed.

"Is he a lawyer?"

"He's a shrink."

"My god, you are wiser," Leo laughed, reaching over to pour more champagne. "Do you want some more?" He poured two full glasses.

"I was just thinking, what's the difference between loving someone or being in love with someone? I mean, the way we were." Ramona felt herself redden, revealing herself so soon. The game with Leo had always been to wait him out. Well, she reminded herself, I don't have anything to lose. She poked at the plastic holding the shells.

"Look, our reservation's in an hour. Should I call and make it later? I mean, if I'm going to answer that question I need some time. I'm no shrink, mujer," Leo laughed.

Ramona hesitated, sensing a trap. Then she changed her mind. "Sure, why not? Make it for seven. I'll put you through a test to see how wise you've gotten." She pressed on the sharp tip of an upraised shell until it poked through the plastic like a tiny, pink nipple. Her own nipples hardened. She wanted to suck the tiny, pink shell-nipple. Instead, she sipped the cool, dry champagne. Years ago, Ramona remembered, when they'd first gotten together, she'd loved sucking Leo's hard, little man's nipples, circling them with her tongue, making him sing higher and higher.

Leo hung up the phone and returned to the couch, sitting opposite her. "This is Felipe's first real girlfriend, isn't she? I mean, she's the first girl I've heard of. I was beginning to wonder about that boy." Leo laughed, but stopped himself, seeing the flicker of anger on Ramona's face. "Anyway, Felipe's shy and sensitive, I suppose, unlike his father." Leo smiled, gauging Ramona's face, appearing boyish, eager to please.

"You're shy and sensitive, Leo. You just keep it a deep, dark secret. Felipe's just more open with it. Honest."

"We are now entering dangerous territory and we've just been together for maybe twenty minutes after six years. That's how it was for us, all right. Dangerous territory." Leo fixed his eyes on the shells on Ramona's lap.

"How else can you get close, Leo?" Ramona looked at her watch. "Look, why don't we go to dinner now? I'm hungry, aren't you?" She forced her tone to be matter-of-fact.

"I just changed the reservation and, besides, it's been a while since I've travelled in dangerous territory."

"Didn't Cathy keep you honest?" Ramona stared the question directly into Leo's eyes. "I guess that's what I was asking you about loving or being in love. . . ."

Leo laughed. "Cathy wasn't a lawyer, Ramona. I got to cross examine her." He paused and stared at Ramona's throat. "Maybe no one's kept me as honest as you. Maybe neither of us could stand it. Hell, I don't know. But I do know I was *in love* with you."

"Did you feel I had power over you?"

Leo laughed loudly. "Damned straight. You could rake me right over the fuckin coals, mujer, and you know it."

Ramona sighed, their old chaotic passion licking at the calmness of her mind. She put her nose into the champagne glass and let the bubbles tease her and then took a sip. "Maybe it's about having power *with* each other rather than power *over* each other. Maybe that's what I want. Now. No, that *is* what I want. I want to be in love *with* someone."

"With the shrink." Leo reminded her.

"His name's David."

Leo stared at the small fire not knowing what to say anymore. He reached over and filled his glass with champagne. "I see you still know how to make a fire. Do you go camping anymore?"

Ramona smiled sadly. "David and I went backpacking in the Sierras this summer. It was really beautiful." She took out the perfect, white, pointy-tipped shell that spiralled into a pink nipple.

"I didn't think I'd miss Felipe so much," Ramona said, staring down at the shell. Her fingers followed the spiral up and down.

Leo looked up, sharply. Her voice took him by surprise; it was so uncharacteristically vulnerable. "I thought you'd be enjoying your freedom and privacy," he said, smiling.

"Don't laugh at me, Leo, okay?" Ramona looked directly into his eyes. "I did really enjoy it for the first few months, but now I really miss the guy." To her intense embarrassment, tears began to fall. One fell on the shell, making it deepen in color. Brighten.

Leo sat next to her. "Do you mind?"

She shook her head no.

He took a shell banded in yellow and turned it in his hand. It was smooth. Perfect. "Do you think you love Felipe, or do you think you're *in love* with Felipe?" Leo stared at the beautiful cream and yellow shell, stroking it between his fingers, enjoying its fragility.

Ramona laughed softly. "Excellent question, excellent." She lay the spiral shell down on the glass table and picked up another. This one was an intense purple, shaped like a fan. "Sorry for the tears, they were spontaneous or something."

"I don't mind." His voice was tender, and the instant he said, "I don't mind," he realized how many times he should've been tender with Ramona, but something had always stopped him. Something out of his control. Something.

Ramona turned the exquisite purple shell over and over. Each side was as beautiful as the other; each side was perfectly matched, held together by its own delicate membrane. "You know, Leo—you know, I think I love Felipe *and* I'm in love with him. I don't think I can choose." Ramona turned her face away, sobbing.

Instinctively, Leo took her into his arms, cradling her. "It's okay," he murmured. "It's okay."

Ramona rested her head against Leo's shoulder as her emotions quieted down. The basket of shells had fallen to the floor, spilling some of them in a beautiful, haphazard design.

"Maybe I'll have to learn to just love him now," she finally said. "You know, knowing how much I'm in love with him. Do you understand?"

"That's what I had to do with you, Ramona. That's exactly what I had to do with you." Tears filled his eyes. "And Felipe."

Ramona looked at him. "Is it true?"

"Yes, it's true." He refused to allow the tears that were beginning to blind him to fall. His eyes stung with the effort of will.

Ramona took him by the hand and asked in a whisper, "Would you make love to me?"

"What about David?" Leo asked, running his fingers up Ramona's arm, still surprised at the intensity of their lovemaking. He travelled her shoulder, her breast, her exposed neck, and her face. Her mouth, her nose, her eyes. There was something in her abandon that satisfied him as no other woman ever had. Yet, he dreaded it; it made him want to surrender, to rest with her. To give her anything she wanted, yes. . . .

"Yes?" Her voice was soft, happy.

"Won't David mind?"

Ramona turned her face and let her eyes take him in. He looked a little older and his eyes didn't seek the center of hers—they never really had—but she recognized him. The body of the man she'd memorized in the years of their loving. He gives me his body but not his soul, the thought came to her, answering her. Her old hunger, her old sorrow, that once ached in her, especially after physical union with him, softened and ate the words: He gives me his body but not his soul.

"He gives me his soul, Leo." As she said it, she realized there was no other answer. She saw a moment of shock on Leo's face and then it closed, becoming a mask of composure and control.

"Are you sorry we made love?" His voice was husky, full of charm, seeking reassurance that he'd hotly deny if cornered.

"You always were a wonderful lover. You always knew my body so well, Leo—I suppose that's why I kept waiting for the intimacy. . . . Well, without us, our lovemaking, no Felipe. No, I'm not sorry for anything, case closed." Ramona shut her eyes and saw David's face clearly, his eyes seeking the center of hers. The ripples of her orgasm with Leo still lulled her, and where once her body remembered hunger, her body now remembered being fed from the time she was in her mother's womb, when her soul, like lightning, joined the mass that she was: the body. David's eyes just reminded her, spoke to the lightning that strikes, unafraid.

She took his hand in hers, but she felt him far away, and she knew he was sorry he was with her. "Without us, Krishna, nothing," she whispered, wondering if he'd heard.

✤ Goddess

CHINA, YELLOW SEA

She watched as her daughter waded in and out of the gentle waves, shells in each hand. Barely two, her pudgy legs collapsed from time to time. How well fed she is, this one. Conceived in the first few months. Disgraceful, like the old days, their tongues clucked. Haven't you heard of birth control? the women's eyes accused her. The men, most, just glanced at her swelling breasts. The belly was a nuisance, but the breasts. . . .

She felt the child kick, a little over four months; a feeble kick, but she felt it. She wondered how much longer she could hide its swelling. Now she wanted it. Why shouldn't I have it, it's mine, now. I feel it moving. Now it's mine.

Her daughter walked toward her, crying. She fell into her lap, reaching for her full breasts. In her father's presence she'd learned to whimper and wait to be fed. With her mother, she touched the cloth where the soft warm milk was hidden and soon it was in her mouth. The taste and feel of her mother's nipple and milk fused in an indescribable ecstasy she'd remember, later, in food, cigarettes, kisses. But, now, the ecstasy flooded her, as her small female body merged with the immense female body of her mother.

She'd tried to explain to her mother: "I just don't want a baby. I want to finish school, go to college, leave the island. I don't *want* to be pregnant!"

"A little late for that, isn't it? Who's the father, he'll marry you. You tell me who it is, your father will make him, you'll see."

"I don't want him to make him. I don't want to get married, and I don't want a baby!" The slap caught her by surprise—she'd never been slapped on the face. She hadn't cried. She turned and walked out the door, leaving it open behind her.

She lay flat in the sand, sifting it between her fingers. The sun was about to set, and she was sorry she hadn't brought her bikini to swim. The water was streaked with fuchsia, mirroring the burning sky. The sun was huge and golden: hot. She felt the sun sigh into the water.

She wasn't sure who the father was. It was her first time, and she'd been drinking the sweet wine cooler, one after the other. She'd taken off her dress, leaving her bikini on, and she'd danced facing the fire. The blasting heat of the bonfire had aroused every inch of her flesh; she'd turned and turned, almost falling into it.

Then facing it, legs spread, moving her hips to the music, a deep, unfamiliar desire stirred, moved inside of her. Making her long to be entered by the fire.

When he took her hand she followed, she remembered. The others must've followed too, but she only remembered him—athletic, muscular. The kind of guy who picked almost any girl he wanted and he'd chosen her. And she'd chosen him. The first time it hurt, but the pain was so mixed with its strange pleasure, she wanted more. Her body was still on fire. "I'm not ready yet, do you want my friend?" She'd nodded yes. And yes to the next. And then she'd had him again, finally.

Exquisite sensations had rippled up and through her vagina, clitoris, womb; when she closed her eyes she saw a volcano erupting, throwing lava and sparks high into the air. She'd smiled, widely, baring her teeth in a wonderful lust, seeing the ancient, slumbering volcano running wild, awake, full of her old power. "Pele," she'd murmured. The boy hadn't heard her and the others had gone back to the fire.

CHINA, YELLOW SEA

Her daughter slept as she carried her; the milk smell, still on her lips, made her smile. He'd be home soon, and she hadn't even started the fire. She liked to cook over an open fire. It reminded her of her grandmother who'd had ten children. Eight had lived, her mother one of them.

"My mother was forced to kill two of her little daughters. Too many daughters in those times made the husband unhappy. Only sons made him happy. I was the eldest daughter. I lived." She remembered her grandmother's eyes; sorrow had been their expression, but at their dark centers a great pride radiated strength. Survival.

She hoped he wasn't home yet as she hurried, but she could go no faster. Her daughter's body slowed her pace—and the daughter within her, who lay crouched and still.

Her heart stopped. A group of people stood by her door. The old woman saw. She saw my swelling. Yes, yes, she told them. She'll receive extra rations for this.

"Oh, Shing Moo," her grandmother's words echoed in her voice, "protect us, Mother, protect us."

Her daughter woke and began to cry for the small pile of shells they'd forgotten at the beach.

HAWAII, MAALAEA BAY

The sun was gone. The wind and waves were still as though the world held its breath. The sky was darkening in its effort to marry the sea.

There were only a few people a little way down the beach. Quickly, she stripped off her clothes and rolled them into a ball, wedging it into the sand. She placed a small coral seashell into her mouth. Its salt made her saliva run, making her hungry, not necessarily for food.

She stood and laughed. She loved the way the twilight wind felt on her naked inner thighs. I will have an abortion. The voice in her mind was firm. Her perfect brown nipples lengthened and became hard as she ran into the barely moving water. As it enveloped her, as she lowered her face into its lush delight, she murmured, "Pele," then ate it, swallowing the shell.

Overhead, biting into the dark purple sky, a slim crescent moon watched over her.

✦ Free Women

"Aren't you glad you didn't bring your husband? Tell the truth, María. Come on, tell the truth!" Marta teased.

María sipped her piña colada and smiled to herself.

"Well, I'm sure as hell glad I didn't," Yolanda laughed. "Look at those macho hunks over there—not bad, not bad." Then she sighed with self-parodying resignation, "Not that I'd do anything. I'm so chicken."

"You aren't chicken. You're faithful. Wish I had someone to be faithful to. Sort of," Consuelo laughed.

"You've never been married, have you?" Marta's voice was languorous. She was finishing her second piña colada. She was in heaven. She'd made it clear to Luis that this was a convention of analysts, therapists, psychiatrists, nothing exciting. Here, in Mexico, by the ocean? Ha! She laughed out loud and put her hand up to get the boy's attention.

"Decadent bitch!" Yolanda teased, with a slight edge in her voice.

"You bet!" Marta shot back. "Do you mind my asking, Consuelo?"

"Too many macho bastards out there, like those gorgeous macho hunks staring at us. So, I guess, I decided to stay single." Consuelo sipped her margarita. It was exactly as she'd ordered it. After she'd sent it back once they got it right. Just seeing her, they got it right. Secretly, the bartender called her La Doctora Puta. So when the busboy brought her drink, the bartender would tell him to take it to La Doctora Puta. Consuelo didn't understand the busboy's wide, cheerful smile. She tipped him well for his smile. He was no more than thirteen, but he had the charm of a man.

"I was married in my twenties. But not ever again, I'll tell you." Marta looked over at Consuelo's long, slender, well-shaped legs and felt her usual envy of women with long slender legs stir. Hers were short with saddle-bags that refused to go away no matter what she did.

"I know my parents think, deep down, that I'm a little sinvergüenza, but, as they well know, I'm too old now for their harmless criticisms. And, besides, I'm the fuckin doctor, right?" Marta laughed loudly, keeping her hand up till she caught the bartender's eye.

"Doesn't Luis want to get married?" María asked. She stared at the bright green lime that floated in her benign, listless mineral water. She stared at her stretch marks from her two children. They aren't ugly enough to hide, she thought, but I'm sure not proud of them. And the stomach never got back to flat again. She remembered her son's comment about her "beer belly" as she'd been relaxing in her bikini. She remembered how much she'd wanted to slap him for being ungrateful to her for the imperfection of her body. The sacrifice of perfection, she told herself, breathing in the perfect day. There were no symposiums till tomorrow. Just me and my beer belly, my brown beer belly, María smiled to herself, letting her breath out softly.

"Oh, he loves me and all that, but I know what lurks beneath that prim Hispanic exterior," Marta laughed sadly. "A Hispanic man who wants to own a woman, a wife, even if you are a doctor and make more than he does. Probably more so because of it, right?" The busboy brought her drink, taking the empty glass. He gave her a small, polite smile as she tipped him. "He's going to be cute when he grows up," Marta said as he retreated to the sound of their appreciative giggles.

"Lecher," Yolanda smiled, imagining his cute brown legs. "Yeah, he'll definitely be hot in a few years like those guys over there staring at us." She was the only one in the group who wore a one-piece bathing suit. She just couldn't bring herself to wear a bikini. All that proper Chicana upbringing hadn't missed its mark. She was short at five foot three and built nicely. She had no stretch marks or children. She often thought what really stopped her from having children was the image of having to spread her legs in front of a bunch of strangers. Even Alfred had to settle with the lights out—and not that he minded. Yolanda was passionate with the lights out. Then he was anyone she desired.

"I have a question for all of you—colleague to colleague." Marta leaned forward, speaking in a low voice. "And I want an honest answer, no bullshit." She looked at her friends and smiled. "You know, the truth." She paused until the only sound was the gentle waves, the sound of glass clinking in the distance, and a radio playing Mexican songs at the bar.

"What's your fantasy of a perfect orgasm?"

"Oh, come on! That's not fair!" Yolanda laughed. "Do you mean right here, right now? I'm supposed to tell all of you my fantasy of a perfect orgasm?"

"I think it's a great idea! Why not? Don't we pry this sort of thing out of our patients? Why not us for a change?" María laughed excitedly.

"Really, why not?" Consuelo joined in María's laughter, but she felt herself blushing high in her cheekbones.

"Because it's personal, pendeja, I'm not your patient," Yolanda answered, laughing.

"Big deal, who'll know? Just us chickens, chicanas. What a bunch of prudes!" Marta pretended intense disappointment.

"Will you tell us yours first?" Consuelo smiled teasingly.

"Sure, why not?" Marta took off her sunglasses and laughed. "But first let's jump in the water. I think this is going to be steamy."

"All those guys are staring. I'll just stay here, go ahead," Yolanda whined.

"I bet you've got the hottest fantasy, Yolanda." Consuelo pulled Yolanda to her feet.

"No doubt," María said, wishing her body was as youthful as Yolanda's. No kids, no belly. She sucked her stomach in, angrily.

"Take this to La Doctora Puta. She wants more," the bartender told the boy.

"She always wants more," the boy smiled.

"They don't seem to notice us," one of the men said. "Maybe they like little boys better." All of them laughed as the boy picked up the drink with a shrug of his shoulders. He liked being included in the men's conversation and their secret ridicule of the pochas. His mother had warned him to stay away from the tourist women. "They're all gringas, no matter what color they are. Mujeres sin vergüenza. They pay you for what's between your legs, just like a man pays a woman! ¡Qué putas!"

He watched La Doctora Puta as she lowered herself into the water. Her body was getting a deep brown; only the edges of her ass betrayed her real color. He wondered how much money she'd pay him. He had no real experience, just some kissing and petting that hadn't gone anywhere. Then they'd left in the night to get away from the soldiers that had taken his father and older brother. He'd been at school when they'd come. When he'd come home his mother's eyes spoke eloquently of her terror. Finally, after many months, they'd come to this place. She took in laundry, sewing, catering to the tourists. Between his job and hers they ate well and lived in peace.

Every night she lit two candles for her husband and her firstborn, wondering where the soldiers had thrown their bodies. She willed herself not to imagine their torture, their screams, their deaths—but sometimes an image of their mutilated bodies surprised her with a terrible violence, and she'd warn her second son: "Cause no trouble. Draw no attention to yourself, ever, hijo, Madre de Dios. . . ."

The boy set the drink down, picking up the dirty one. He noticed the others were almost empty, so he waited for them to return. La Doctora Puta turned toward him. She adjusted her bikini top unselfconsciously. She has nice ones, he thought. I'd like a motorcycle, a black one. A big black one with silver and a nice motor. He watched her breasts bounce as she approached. My father's dead and I have nothing. He smiled at her and she smiled back at him, but, quickly, she looked away and began to towel herself, aware of his eyes on her.

I wonder if he's a virgin? No, I shouldn't even think it, Consuelo told herself firmly.

I have nothing, the boy repeated to himself, watching her spread oil to her face, neck, the tops of her breasts. Then the other women came, giving him instructions. He always had to force himself not to laugh at their Spanish. It was forced, self-conscious, too perfect, like from books. Even the one who acted like their women wanted a margarita. Hers was the Spanish that sounded natural like spoken language. They were laughing as he walked away. "Gringas," he muttered.

The boy returned with their fresh drinks, dropping a napkin in Consuelo's lap. He'd written on it, "I like you, Señora." She read it and looked up at him, completely undone for a moment. He licked his upper lip, staring at her, and then he smiled like a boy seeking approval, with the charm and intent of a confident man. When the boy was gone, Consuelo wiped the sheen of sweat from her face, neck, and breasts with the note—I like you, Señora. She tore the napkin into small shreds and reminded Marta of her promise to be first.

All of them giggled, sounding like teenagers at a pajama party with a joint or two being passed around—the incense lit so the vigilant parents wouldn't know. Their bodies felt young and alive with sexual curiosity, and, miraculously, they felt no guilt—thirteen, fourteen, fifteen. . . .

Marta cleared her throat, laughed nervously, and, settling into her reclining chair, she surrendered her body to the hot afternoon sun. Then, with an unusually graceful gesture, she placed a small shell on her dream eye. Marta had suggested they all find one shell to stimulate their dream eye for their perfect fantasy. This could be healing, she thought. She imagined its light, subtle weight made her dream eye quiver, almost itch.

"Girls, if I get too steamy tell me to shut up, okay?" No one answered. They were all oiled, drinks within reach, turning browner by the minute and glad they weren't first in their little game. Marta shut her eyes and her voice became a dreamy monotone.

"I'm in a meadow, it's springtime, warm but not hot, and the meadow's filled with flowers, flowers of every color and the softest green, green grass. I'm wearing a flimsy spring dress with silk panties and bra, a golden silk, which can be seen through the dress, and the wind's blowing through me as though I'm naked." She actually felt the spring wind and opened her eyes for a second to see if the warm sea and hot sand still surrounded her. She felt languid, sensual.

"It's in the mountains, there's a creek close by, and then I hear voices, a woman and a man. They're like twins, only he's blonde and she's raven-haired, black, black hair with dark sensual eyes. His eyes are ocean blue, deep blue, powerful. Both of their eyes are extremely powerful, and they're both physically beautiful. Their combined presence is almost overwhelming me." Marta paused, sipping her drink, and lay back down. She rubbed her oily belly once, enjoying her own caress, then she held absolutely still.

"They tell me together, in one voice, 'Take off your dress.' I do. Then he takes off my gold silk bra and his hands are both soft and strong. He takes my breast into his mouth and twirls his tongue around my nipple and he sucks it and licks my entire breast with his tongue and then back to my nipple, teasing it, twirling it with his tongue, and it's like, it's like I'm having an orgasm. He takes the other one in his mouth and I can't stand it. I fall down onto the flowers, and I feel the woman slip by gold silk panties off, licking my belly, pressing her face into my belly, circling my pubis with her wet tongue. He kisses my lips, filling my mouth with his thick tongue, then my breasts again and again. My mouth, eyes, cheeks, eyelids, everything from the breasts up belong to him, and the woman owns the clitoris as she strokes it with her tongue so softly, yet firmly."

Marta's breath caught. She raised her leg, squeezing herself, feeling shudders of pleasure run through her body.

"I come and come in swirling colors, flowers, smells, a multitude of sensations and there's no boundary, no place where I can say the orgasm begins here, ends here, it's one continuous, rolling, flowing orgasm. . . . like the meadow.

Her friends were silent, each one in her own meadow.

"Then I feel the man penetrate me, and for a moment I want to say no, stop, no, but his possession is complete, his hands clutch me, and his thrusts, deep into my womb, drive the orgasm back into me, back to a kind of frenzied, yet sharper focus. A kind of gathering of my power, yes. Now I want his sperm, all of it. All of it is mine." Marta couldn't help laughing, softly, with pleasure.

"And the woman?" María asked with admiration. Marta had definitely set the tone and though she felt aroused by the fantasy, she suddenly dreaded she had none of her own.

"The woman's mine too." Marta burst out laughing. "I assume, fellow shrinks, that all of this is highly confidential, right?" She smiled at her friends, wondering how she'd conjured up that meadow, those twins, and missing it at the same time.

"Of course it is. It's absolutely confidential, sister shrink," Yolanda laughed. "What an incredible fantasy."

"Look, we could all analyze that one. It's really healthy, Marta," Consuelo said. "The man *and* the woman. Perfect."

"Plus, it's hot," María giggled.

"Exactly what I was getting to. Let's not analyze our fantasies—that's what we do for a living. Let's just keep it going, okay? You next, María." Consuelo smiled, sipping her drink. "Drink slowly, so you-know-who doesn't sneak up on us."

"We're speaking English, remember?" Yolanda rolled onto her stomach. She glanced at the men at the bar and one of them smiled at her. She smiled back and immediately regretted it. She sipped her drink and laid her head on the soft beach pillow. The sun engulfed her. She imagined taking the bathing suit off and oiling herself, everything. My back, my ass, my legs, my thighs, she thought. Someone else would have to do it. Yolanda smiled as María started to speak.

"I'm in a room of mirrors—walls, ceiling, floor. Well, I'm naked, laying on a giant black futon with colored cushions. There are cushions everywhere—blue, red, purple, yellow, lime, rainbow pillows, name it." María paused, trying to get the image sharper. She saw her belly, slightly rounded, her hips and thighs overweight, yet full and somehow sensual. She smiled at the emptiness of the room—just herself and the mirrors.

"There seems to be a natural light, but I don't see any windows. There's music playing, Brazilian music. I look up at the ceiling and spread my legs and watch myself touch my labia. I spread my labia, placing my fingers inside my wetness. I caress my clitoris, slowly, with my right hand; my left hand squeezes my nipples hard and soft—a door in the mirror to my left opens and a beautiful man walks toward me. He's smiling at me. He asks, 'May I join you?' His voice is so friendly and pitched low, inviting. I nod my head, yes."

María tapped the shell on her forehead. Maybe it really works, she mused, seeing the beautiful man put his tongue in her mouth, in and out, rhythmically, the way she liked it. "Now he's fucking my mouth with his tongue." María became embarrassed and laughed.

"Oh, come, we're all grown women, keep it rolling," Marta complained. "It's just starting to get good, mujer." Marta's shell was still perched on her dream eye, so she imagined she was right there in the room with María.

María took a sip of her drink and continued. "Now a door in the mirror to my right opens and a beautiful blonde man walks through. By the way, the first one has black hair."

"I know," Marta murmured.

"The blonde man lays to my right, placing his penis on my thigh. It's hard, he wants me. He begins to suck my breasts. One, then the other, moaning. The black-haired man continues to fuck my mouth, and I'm beginning to moan with pleasure like I never have before. I mean, ever—they both want me."

"Holy shit," Yolanda couldn't help saying. "I'm getting hot just hearing about it." The other women giggled; they felt the same.

"A door in the mirror behind me opens and a man with red hair lays to my left and places his penis on my thigh as he begins to stroke my belly, down to my thighs, my knees, my calves, back up, and he finds my clitoris. Now I'm screaming, mutely, in my throat. A beautiful black man comes through a door in the mirror in front of me and falls down, immediately, to eat my pussy. The men begin to moan loudly, in unison, like an ancient chant. The black-haired man puts his penis in my mouth and I want it; I suck it. The men to my side caress me and suck my breasts. The penis in my mouth never goes in too far, doesn't gag me. I'm eating him, the black man is eating me. I come with unbelievable explosions, my body's out of control. I crawl, I writhe, I cry, I laugh. Then each man fucks me, and each one is distinct, different, unique. My vagina continues to convulse, sending messages to my womb straight up to my brain and back to my toenails. I watch each man as we fuck in the mirrors, on top of me, me straddling, on our sides, like dogs, standing, sitting face to face. Then they surround me, kneeling, they touch me with their hands, telling me, 'You're beautiful, You're beautiful,' over and over."

"Jesus, these fantasies must be repressed. They're looming up, in full color, right in our faces," Consuelo laughed.

"No analysis, remember?" Yolanda reminded her.

"Yes, please, no analysis. This is wonderful." Marta's voice was soft.

María wept with a strange joy. Each man was so vivid to her, so beautiful and each one thought she was beautiful. *She was beautiful.* Joy. Strange, strange joy.

"You should see their books, a stack of them. They're supposed to be doctoras, but you'd never know, the way they lay out there in the sun with nothing on," Lupe told the other maid.

"You wonder if they have a man. My husband wouldn't let me go about by myself."

"Only to work, I know." Lupe sighed. "Maybe if we grew up in the North we'd be here with our books."

"And the children?"

"Maybe we'd have no children."

"I'd rather be a mother than a whore."

"They're not whores, they're, as they say, free women." Lupe was startled at the sound of the words, *mujeres libres.* She laughed. "¡Las pochas sin vergüenza!"

"For me, I'll take my husband and my children. We have a good life here, Lupe. The work is plentiful. And, besides, you have a good man, so good looking too. And your two children are perfect."

"What you say is true." Lupe smiled. "But between you and I, I've always wanted to read books. As a girl I imagined writing them. I used to write poems." Lupe's voice dropped to a whisper. "Of course, I never showed anyone."

"Do you still have them? I'd like to see them. You could read them to me. I'd like that." Her friend's shy longing touched her unexpectedly.

"They're all gone, lost. I wrote them when I was a girl . . ."

"Write some more. Show them to me. I can't imagine what you'd say, but I'd like to know."

Lupe laughed, putting her hand on her friend's shoulder. "Maybe I will, but it's been so long, and what will I write? After all, I'm a wife and mother now . . ."

"So? You're not dead!"

They laughed softly, lowering their heads to the afternoon sun and walked, arm in arm, toward their homes.

"I see you have your bag of shells for the children to paint. Are they selling?" she asked Lupe.

"They are so ethnic, pet shells," Lupe imitated the gringa's tone in her accented English.

"Qué ethnic, muchacha, how much do they charge?" she laughed.

"I'm embarrassed to say, it's like stealing. But they do make them cute. They've even begun to glue feathers on them, como los indios."

"Qué chula, save one for me. One never knows about the things children make. They could bring luck. Write a poem about luck, Lupe, for me." She hoped the baby would be clean when she got home and that no accidents had occurred. To hope he'd be home was too much. She knew he was at the cantina.

Lupe squeezed her friend's arm. "I will do it." Her words made her heart race with happiness. She would write a poem for Juanita.

"Did you ever have an orgasm like that?" Yolanda asked. "You don't mind my asking, do you?"

María took the shell off of her forehead and adjusted the lounge to a semisitting position. "In the beginning, when I used to have more than one lover at a time, in my early twenties when I was sampling men, I did." María smiled sadly. "And in the first years of my marriage when I thought I was, oh you know, beautiful. Now, I have an orgasm, period. You know."

"I've never had an orgasm like you described." Yolanda lowered her voice. "Not ever."

María laughed softly. "Well, I've never made love to four men at the same time, so why don't you take a shot at it. Don't hold back."

"You give me courage," Yolanda smiled. "Do you all promise not to tell anyone what's heard here today, cross your heart and hope to die, stick a needle in your eye?"

"Stick a needle in my eye."

"Hope to die."

"My lips are sealed."

"Liars!" Yolanda laughed as she lay down on her stomach, pressing the small translucent shell into her forehead so hard it hurt. "Okay, I'm on a stage, kind of dimly lit. I'm laying on an air mattress reading a book." Yolanda paused, trying to see the scene, herself in the scene, as clearly as possible. She laughed with embarrassment, pulling her long, dark hair to one side. The sun felt good on the soft, exposed flesh of her neck.

"Okay, I'm wearing this little girl's dress, full and flouncy, with a white petticoat. I'm wearing white cotton panties and I'm barefoot. I know there're people in the audience. I can almost hear them breathe, but I can't see anyone. An older man, in his fifties, walks toward me from the darkness. He's good looking with full, gray hair. He's wearing a suit and a tie and he looks well built. He's handsome but fatherly. 'I've come to make you happy,' he tells me. 'You must do everything I say.' His words scare me, but they also excite me. I just look at him. 'Close the book. If you're very good, I'll give you anything you want, later.' He takes my dress off and carefully folds it, laying it to one side. I'm not wearing a bra and my nipples look pink and girlish, though I look like myself now. He takes my nipples in his mouth, murmuring, 'I bet you like this,' over and over. I'm surprised at the pleasure I feel, but I don't want to let him know. He continues to ask me if I like what he's doing to me—he stays fully dressed. I don't mind that he's fully dressed, I rather prefer it that way for some reason." Yolanda paused.

"Like I'd rather not see his body, his erection, if he has one. I can't tell. He slips his hand into my panties and begins to stroke me softly, very softly, saying, 'You like this, you like this . . .' My breath is speeding up and my skin feels like it's starting little fires wherever he strokes me. I want to move, but then he'll know that I like what he's doing, so I lay absolutely still. 'Now I'm going to see what you taste like,' he tells me. He pokes his tongue out at me and smiles, continuing to stroke my neat, folded labia with his smooth, careful fingers. I'm burning up, but I don't move."

Yolanda's breath caught at what she saw next. She felt like masturbating as she spoke, but, of course, that was impossible. She took a deep, full breath. "He lowers my panties to my thighs and slightly parts my legs and he begins to lick my clitoris, making no sound with his mouth. He's so polite, he's exquisite. He's holding my hips between his open palms and he lifts his head, 'I'm not stopping until you come.' His tongue is rhythmic, soft like a puppy's—his hands begin to rotate my hips, making me move. The lights begin to brighten, slightly, but I don't mind. Someone in the audience, a woman, asks, 'Do you think she'll come?' over and over. 'I know you like this,' the man says and then continues to lick my clitoris. I'm writhing around but I refuse to make any noise. The lights get brighter as I begin to come, feeling his tongue lick my perfect little clitoris. I shut my eyes, just feeling his tongue, the sensation of my orgasm radiates to every part of my body, and the light explodes like the sun as I scream that I love it, I love it better than anything in the world . . . the man holds me, cradles me, 'I know you do,' he tells me. And it's so fucking wonderful to come this way, just for me. The audience begins to clap, loudly." Yolanda laughed at her own ending.

The women clapped, laughing with her.

"Oh, please don't clap, how embarrassing! What if my husband heard this? He'd croak!" Yolanda laughed louder and her eyes began to tear as she turned onto her back, dropping the shell. It lay on the sand, merging almost perfectly, as though Yolanda had never touched it. "Next fantasy, next fantasy!" And then the word *fantasy* made her sad.

"My turn, last and worst, right?" Consuelo giggled. "Yours were all so great, I'm feeling intimidated, like all the great fantasies are taken."

"Oh, come on, Consuelo, you must have a secret fantasy up your you-know-what," Marta teased.

"You-know-what?" María repeated. "You mean her sleeve?" She kept a straight face, making Consuelo burst into a fit of laughter.

"Okay, okay, I'll tell . . ."

"Wait, Consuelo, the spy's returning," Marta laughed, indicating the boy walking toward them. They all began to giggle.

As he stood next to Consuelo waiting for them to order, he dropped a note into her lap: "Do you like me?" Consuelo stood up to stretch and adjust her bathing suit. Quickly, she handed him her shell and smiled at him, whispering, "Tonight."

As he walked toward the bar with the word *tonight* ringing in his head, he held the shell tightly in his hand and imagined himself driving the silver motorcycle. He could feel his hands grip the black rubber handlebars that would take him wherever he wanted to go. Wherever he wanted to go. And it would belong to him.

He placed the fresh drinks next to them, carefully. La Doctora Puta was speaking to the other putas in English. Just the sound, the droning, flat sound of the language bored him. It didn't rise or fall like his own language. It has no flesh, he thought. No blood, no heart. He smiled, revealing his white, hungry teeth.

". . . but I have to teach him how to satisfy me, he's still a virgin. So, I tell him to lay next to me. 'Show me your tongue,' I tell him. . . ."

"Do you honestly think there's any nineteen-year-old virgins around?" Yolanda interjected.

"It's my fantasy, right?"

"Come on, Yolanda, be quiet," María laughed. "She's right though. You'd have to snatch a twelve-year-old to get a virgin these days."

"Maybe the busboy's a virgin," Marta couldn't resist adding. She'd noticed the boy staring at Consuelo with interest—and she couldn't help thinking Consuelo noticed the boy as well.

"Never. Do you forget that I'm a child psychiatrist?" Consuelo smiled, spreading her legs to the hot Mexican sun. She wanted her innermost thighs to darken, to burn. She wondered, suddenly, what it felt like to have your heart cut out of your body. Would you be able to see it, for a moment, in the priest's bloody hands? She shivered with fear and excitement and continued to lie to her friends, so leisurely, in English.

✣ Sabra

The red-tailed hawk circled, widely, in the morning sky. The coastal fog was beginning to lift and the sweep of the distant hills were emerging into thin spring sunlight. Judith brought her coffee out to the sunlight, still unable to believe she was in California. They'd paid her way and accepted her for this residency on the strength of her slides, her few exhibitions. They considered her to be a promising young painter.

Judith looked older in the morning light; older than thirty-two. Her short hair, cut close to her head, her old sweat shirt and jeans, the cynical expression she wore in public, as well as in private, made her look like an old soldier. She looked for movement in the deep green hills, for trailing smoke, for anything unusual. She looked back at the enormous barn. This would be her studio for six months. Another artist was due to arrive tomorrow. He would occupy the other studio in the barn.

I've been to war, Judith thought. I've watched people die. My side and theirs. She lit her third cigarette of the day and held the smoke in her lungs till it burned her to her satisfaction. Begrudgingly, she let it go and watched it mingle into the cool air. Why does it frighten me to sleep in this quiet place? "California," she said out loud and took another sip of her black coffee.

Judith looked up to the writer's house, as they called it, and didn't envy their close quarters. Writers just need a room with their desk, paper, and fingers. She smiled. Me, I need room to splash around, mix paints, surround myself with preliminary sketches. I need room to create. No, I wouldn't want to be boxed in with the writers, but the darkness, the silence last night was almost unbearable. She broke into a sweat as the unfamiliar fear clutched her. Angrily, she smoothed her hair from her face with both hands and closed her eyes to the sweet, yellow sunlight.

"I am a Sabra."

Judith opened her eyes and saw the dissolving fog over the coastline creating diamonds of light. Again, the diamonds of light, the triangles, she realized. These shapes were almost constantly present in her work. They disturbed her. They irritated her, as though they had a message she couldn't decipher. They'd begun to appear in a portrait she'd painted after the time at one of the many borders and skirmishes she'd taken part in. They appeared, almost invisibly, like subtle lights, little triangles, the diamond lights, behind the head. She remembered the urge to paint them floating out of her friend's mouth, like words. Judith had suppressed the urge immediately, but allowed them to stay in the background, floating, giving the painting a pleasant surprise of an unknown quality. Abstraction.

Judith blinked her eyes, forcefully, but the diamond lights threatened to blind her. She shifted her gaze toward the green hills closer to her and the diamond lights receded. Still no movement, not even the hawk, though the sound of birds singing and calling surrounded her. Why is it so silent here at night? Judith looked at her hands. They were small but strong. Like death, she thought involuntarily, shuddering.

She leapt to her feet and went into the studio kitchen, the one she'd share with the arriving artist, a sculptor from Germany, and got a second cup of coffee. She knew the diamonds, the triangles, would find their way into the new painting. Judith wondered how she and the German would get along. She knew her parents wouldn't, to this day, live under the same roof with a German; her father lost his parents, both sets of grandparents, to the concentration camps. He and his sisters had been sent away, in time, to a family in Sweden. Her mother's brother, ten at the time, had been picked up walking home, the Jewish star sewn on his coat, never seen again. Her family finally fled after months of trying to find him, discreetly, through French friends. He'd come to Judith's mind, sometimes, during the soldier's training. Never again, Reuben, she'd tell him silently. Never, ever again, as she bayoneted the targeted figure through its vital organs.

Judith walked into her studio, and, again, she approved of the morning light streaming through the wraparound sliding glass doors and the large bubble skylight. Already she could see the diamond lights wanting to appear in the trunks of the trees, the sky's immense horizon, this country they call California. Judith smiled at the diamonds slyly. Tomorrow the German comes, she thought. Maybe I'll give you to him as a gift. She laughed out loud at the irrationality of it. It appealed to her abstract sense of order. The premonition of it, the abstract sense of order, always made her shiver violently though the studio was almost too warm. She opened one of the sliding doors wide.

Today she'd walk down to the creek where the trees grew thickly. She'd never seen redwoods before and loved them immediately. She'd take her sketch pad and pencils. The redwoods frightened her a little; they felt old and silent. Their presence, in a group, seemed to create an unnerving silence, and though it attracted her, it, the silence, also challenged her to penetrate what she thought the silence held: a secret.

The German will make this barn a little less lonely, Judith told herself. Maybe he'll even be good looking. She laughed out loud again. A sudden wind, fresh smelling from the sea, swept some papers to the cement floor. Yes, she thought, walking to the open window, spotting the hawk—she imagined its muscles, its wings, its terrible control in the wind that enabled it to fly—yes, maybe he'll take the diamonds. Maybe they're his.

"This is too, too irrational, Judith," she murmured. But saying it made her feel light and free. She turned on some music and began her usual ritual of stalking her painting, until the moment she touched the canvas with the first stroke of her brush.

"What part of Germany are you from, Frank?"

Judith watched the writer flirt with her new roommate. She cringed at the thought of this woman waking up in the studio next to her. She could imagine her loud squeals of passion, her high laughter ruining her mornings when she worked.

"I'm from Berlin. Would you pass me that bottle of cabernet? This meal is so very good." Frank smiled at the cook/hostess/den mother of the artists, Janine. He was good looking, sophisticated, at ease with himself, and his accent lent to his charm. It wasn't harsh, but soft, to Judith's surprise.

"Will you be needing a model?" The writer was letting him know she meant business. Judith groaned inwardly.

Frank laughed, including the woman in his charm. "If I do, I'll let you know. That's very thoughtful of you, Karen."

Judith picked up her plate and got to her feet. "Janine, the meal was perfect. Are you sure you don't want help with these dishes?"

"No, no. Just rinse it and leave it in the sink for the dishwasher. Going to bed so soon?" Janine felt utterly comfortable with her third glass of wine.

"I took a long walk today, further than I meant to. Good night to all." Judith swept the room with her eyes, avoiding contact with Frank's eyes. As she stepped outside, she looked down to the barn and its small patch of light, actually a floodlight, she'd left on to guide her back. In the darkness, the absolute darkness that descended here, it was a small patch of light. For an instant she wanted to go back inside with the others, but she made herself move toward the steps off the patio toward the dirt path that led to the light.

The door opened and shut behind her. "Do you want company?" Frank called, walking toward her. "How in hell do you find your way back? I can't even see your face clearly."

Judith laughed quietly. "Are you afraid?"

"Yes. But together we'll be brave, no?" He laughed with her. "I brought a supply of wine for the exiles. Are you really going to bed?"

His face was becoming clear in the darkness. There was no doubt that he was German. He's almost typical, Judith thought. He's so very blonde. He probably has very little body hair. The thought made her smile with sudden curiosity. She remembered her parents and answered herself, This is the country of California.

"I really am tired from that walk. . . ." Judith stumbled on a rock and Frank caught her, nearly breaking the wine bottles.

"You haven't even unpacked yet. Why don't we go to my studio? Are you really going to create in here? Sculptings, I mean." Judith's eyes ran critically over Frank's luggage and a huge carton, and then Frank himself.

"You're cynical, world-weary, I like that in a woman. Sure, let's go to your studio. The wine doesn't care where it's poured." Within seconds they were in her adjoining studio.

"And you're not cynical living in Berlin?"

"To the contrary, I'm cheerful." Frank smiled widely, as if to prove his point. He poured the wine and handed her a glass.

"Do you think we're going to get along here in the barn?" Judith took the glass without looking into his transparent blue German eyes.

"One of the writers, up at the house, has his eye on you, you know," Frank teased her.

"You already have a model." Judith smiled past him at one of her drawings. "Do you think we're going to get along? I'm from Israel or didn't you know?" She met his gaze and held it. She saw no aggression in his blue, blue eyes. In fact, she felt the pleasure he took in staring at her. She shifted her eyes to a light that came from his right ear. His long blonde hair covered his ears, but Frank had smoothed his hair back from his face, exposing an earring.

"We're artists, aren't we? Aren't artists supposed to transcend history, unite the ununitable? Do you mind that I'm German?" Frank's voice stiffened slightly, but his face remained sensually watchful.

"I don't know if I mind. My family has a vivid memory of their family lost in the," she paused, unaccountably embarrassed to say it to him, a stranger, and a German.

"In the Holocaust. Part of my education was visiting the former sites of the concentration camps, you know." He took a sip of his wine. "I'm sorry your family suffered."

Judith saw that the light in his ear was a diamond earring shaped like a triangle. She stopped breathing for a moment. The diamond of light. "Does your family talk about that time?" her words rushed out forcefully.

"Never. Not to me, anyway. I can never figure out if they're ashamed of what the Germans did or that Germany lost the war, you know? But on that subject one always felt shame from them, floating, undefined, or at least unexplained, to me." Frank liked her short, boyish hair, her lack of make-up, the absence of flirtation in her manner. A certain deadly *calm*, he mused, looking at her. Women usually have a more, oh, jittery energy, more eager to please. This one looks away at her leisure or right through me.

"I see." Judith's voice had an edge of anger in it.

"I've never killed anyone," Frank burst into defensive laughter. "I just happened to be born in Germany."

"Do you honestly feel you just happened to be born in Germany?"

"I certainly didn't plan it. Here, have some more wine." He passed her a full glass. "Do you believe me that I've never killed anyone?" He saw her face gather itself closed. It reminded him of his uncle, but on her it seemed a charming testimony to feminine strength. A kind of invulnerability that he admired in women. He thought of his mother's face—all sorrow, remorse, guilt.

Frank finished his glass of wine and said, "I suppose I should leave and let you go to sleep, which is why you left the others early, no?" He stood to leave.

"Please don't go," Judith blurted out to stop his gesture to leave. It was too late to take the words back, so she continued, trying to regain her composure, her usual aura of control. Judith met Frank's eyes and glanced at the diamond light in his ear, then back to his eyes. "I'm not that tired now, not anymore. Pour me another glass of wine."

"I'll have to open a new bottle."

"Okay."

"Do you have any candles? This studio lighting can be so harsh at night."

Judith brought two lit candles from the kitchen, and Frank turned the lights off. They sat on a patch of rug by the wide expanse of windows. It was clear. The fog hadn't rolled in yet and the stars were crowded in the black sky.

"Do you know that I haven't looked at the stars since I've arrived? It's either been foggy, or I've gone straight to sleep," Judith said, looking up at the clusters of glittering stars. "I'm glad you're here." Her voice became soft, shy.

"Even if I'm German?" Frank smiled at her as he moved the distance between them and kissed her lightly on the lips. He began to pull away, but she held onto him, penetrating his mouth with her tongue, breathing him in. He liked aggressive women. He liked to be made love to, and he knew he would enjoy seeing the woman in her unfold and surface in the orgasm he would give her with his tongue. He loved the feel of her strong body. Everywhere he touched her she was solid, except for her breasts where she was hot and sweaty. And her soft, full thighs.

A waning crescent moon gave them light. Judith touched his diamond triangle with her fingers as her orgasm mounted and mounted, to the place she would kill to come. Where nothing could stand in the way of her orgasm. Like dying, like killing, the thought flashed through her mind like lightning.

His orgasm had been slow and gentle. Luxurious, filling her to the opening of her womb. "Beautiful, yes, beautiful," he'd said as she'd filled herself with him, straddling him, staring at him with her steady eyes. She'd thrown her head back a few times, but she'd always come back to meet his eyes.

He closed his eyes when his orgasm erupted, but he knew she was watching him dissolve.

Now, as her orgasm overtook her, enveloped her, melted and shook her violently, spiralling her blind, ecstatic, she was helpless, utterly helpless. Then in the eye of the void—before birth, before death—she shut her eyes, tightly, her breath coming fast and hard as she labored. Through the dark tunnel came the deafening silence, the explosion of diamond lights, the tiny triangles growing larger, the diamond lights blinding her, and far, far away the shrill sounds of screaming. Screams, screams, soul-shattering screams in the harsh diamond light.

> The dark-haired boy is no older than
> Reuben. My mother's brother, Reuben,
> is killed again. Reuben will
> be killed again and again and
> again.
> The stone hits me and I turn, blindly,
> and kill a child, a child, a
> child, as the women scream, my
> mother screams, the child is dead
> again.

Frank placed a cold washcloth on her face. Water dripped from the edges like tears, down her cheeks. "Judith, Judith, are you all right? Come on, wake up! Judith, Come on, wake up!"

Her eyes flew open. "I'm okay, really, I'm okay. It's so intense sometimes is all . . ." Judith began to sob. "Show me your earring, show me . . ."

Frank lay down next to her, pushing his hair to one side. He stroked her body, softly. "Tell me what's wrong."

She looked at his earring, the diamond triangle shining in the darkness between them, and she wanted to say, "I am a Sabra and I have killed."

"Tell me what's wrong, tell me," Frank whispered as he stroked her body, her face, smearing her tears, but she remained silent.

Finally, Judith spoke. "May I have it?"

"The earring, you mean?"

"Yes, may I?"

Frank smiled in the darkness. The waning crescent had set long ago and the last candle was extinguished. "I'll trade with you, Aphrodite."

"Why do you call me Aphrodite?"

"She's a Goddess I admire and you remind me of her."

Judith sighed deeply like a woman accepting a grief that no mourning can ever end. The acceptance of the unacceptable.

Frank took off his diamond earring and handed it to her. "And yours, Aphrodite?"

Judith removed an earring and handed it to him.

He held the tiny silver earring, shaped like a scallop. As he placed it in his ear he said, "Shells are sacred to Aphrodite. Thank you, Aphrodite of the sea." Frank kissed Judith, nibbling her lips.

"Why do you call me Aphrodite?" Judith murmured, weighed down by Reuben's lost look: *Children don't die.*

Frank touched both of her ears—the triangle, the shell—"Because, beautiful woman, Aphrodite has the power of life and death. Because . . ."

Judith pulled him toward her, covering his mouth with hers. "The child, the child, oh, the child . . ."

❖ Empty

The white buzzing sound wipes me clean.
I could be a leaf floating in the wind
or in a stream. I could be a lea
gathering in a twig. But I'm not.
I'm the white buzzing sound. The
terrible white light men make.
Their machine that hates me.
I remember nothing. Nothing.
And I smile at nothing.
They think I'm better.
I remember nothing.
Nothing.
I long for the comfort
of darkness, the long
black tunnel where the light
of memory flickers at the end. . . .
The white buzzing sound wipes me clean.

❖

Annie ran into the kitchen, without her usual knock, looking for my daughter: "Is Clara here?" She was out of breath and her eyes were panic-stricken.

"Is anything wrong, Annie?" Annie, like my daughter, is sixteen—but Annie has a body like Jayne Mansfield. She wears at least six to ten ear-rings on each ear and one in her nose. It doesn't look outlandish. It becomes her, in fact. Today, she's wearing a sheer-looking tie-up-the-front peasant blouse, with beautiful ribbons dangling from it, and a full, colorful peasant skirt. She's barefoot, but it's summer and warm.

"I had to hitchhike here. My father wouldn't drive me." Annie's voice trembled with anger and excitement. "You'd think this county would have bus lines connecting these stupid little towns. Is Clara here?"

"She tried to call you this morning, but no one answered."

"He unplugs it when his girlfriend's over, which is why he wouldn't drive me."

"Clara had to go in for dress rehearsals today. You know, the play she's in. Do you want some tea or something?"

Annie flashed me a look of sad resentment, and I could feel her thinking, Clara has a *real* mother. "May as well since I'm here, thanks."

I began fixing the tea and a couple of sandwiches. "Doesn't your father worry about you hitchhiking? He's a psychiatrist, right? That's what Clara told me. . . ."

"Yeah, he's a shrink and all." Annie threw herself into a chair. "I almost got raped coming over here." She spread her hands on her lap and stared at the beautiful ribbons falling toward them, but not quite touching. "I started screaming and jumped out at a fucking stop sign."

She looked like a fairy-tale little girl, barefoot, with ribbons reaching down to her lap, her golden hair curling down to her shoulders. A fairy-tale little girl, with an extraordinary woman's body, at the mercy of a dark and evil, all-powerful king.

> The white buzzing sound wipes me clean.
> I could be a leaf floating in the wind
> or a stream. I could be a leaf
> gathering in a twig. But I'm not.
> I'm the white buzzing sound. The
> terrible white light men make.
> Their machine that hates me.

I remember nothing. Nothing.
And I smile at nothing.
They think I'm better.
I remember nothing.
Nothing.
I long for the comfort
of darkness, the long
black tunnel where the light
of memory flickers at the end. . . .
The white buzzing sound wipes me empty.

❖

I thought she was going to cry, but when I tried to touch her she pulled away from me. I could see Annie willing herself to composure, so I turned to pour the boiling water into the waiting cups.

"Was the guy alone?"

"Yeah."

"Do you remember the license, the make of car?"

Annie's eyes looked panic-stricken again. "I'm not calling the cops. That's all the proof my father needs."

"Proof of what? It's not your fault that someone tried to rape you, it's really not. But promise me you won't hitchhike again, that's cutting it too close, Annie." I looked out to the open field. Living here, I sometimes forgot that the usual violence continued. But just beyond, on the highway—I thought of my daughter. She has a ride home tonight. I looked at Annie, the sheer, beautiful peasant blouse cut a little low, the swell of her full breasts. . . . she shouldn't wear that outfit and hitchhike. . . . she shouldn't hitchhike at all. Clara's nowhere that developed, I thought with relief.

"My father always says I'm going to end up like my mother." Annie squeezed her tea bag, placing it beside her cup. "She was a, pardon the expression, a slut, and now she's crazy. Like every time my family has a get-together—my grandparents and all—they all look at me like I might go off my rocker right before their eyes." Annie laughed and continued talking while eating her sandwich.

"I even look like her a lot. Only I'm not repressed the way she was. I mean, my grandfather was a real Victorian. He owns an antique business. You should see some of the stuff he gives me. Well, actually, I've earned it working for him in the store during vacations. It's really ritzy, in Mill

Valley. Anyway, that's her father. My other grandfather's a real winner—he thinks my father should tranquilize me. Yeah, actually, just put me on tranquilizers because I've always had so much energy. I say he's just a jealous, control-oriented, patriarchal dinosaur, which makes my father fume, though I know he secretly agrees with me and all, 'cause he can't stand him either. I mean, I don't even drink and everyone wants to put me on *drugs* and all. . . ."

I interrupted. "Annie, why do you think your mother's a so-called slut and crazy? Don't you think that's a pretty harsh judgment?" Annie swung her beautiful golden hair to one side of her face as though to hide. "Do you mind my asking?"

Annie looked up and held my eyes. "She slept around when they were married. She even went to bars and picked up strange men and my father caught her and all. Clara says she's Mayan. Is that true and all?"

"It's true. Both my family and Clara's father's family were from Mexico, central Mexico. . . ."

"Where's Clara's father, anyway?" Annie sat forward in the chair as though she was preparing to run.

I smiled at Annie to reassure her and thought of my ex-husband. To my surprise his face, his memory, was as clear as a photograph. "I'm sure you know we're divorced. He lives in San Francisco. You know, when we used to fight, he used to accuse me of being crazy. At first it used to hurt my feelings and make me cry, but then it started really pissing me off." I laughed, seeing Annie's face register amazement.

"He really started saying that kind of thing when he felt himself losing control—over me, that is. Maybe losing what he thought was control made *him* feel crazy, right?"

"Did you ever *feel* crazy?" Annie whispered.

I paused, staring out at the steer who'd wandered into view, grazing on the thick, oat hay that I'd seeded the previous fall. "Yes, I did. But only when I didn't trust my own truth. What I really knew to be true."

> *The white buzzing sound wipes me clean.*
> *I could be a leaf floating in the wind*
> *or in a stream. I could be a leaf*
> *gathering in a twig. But I'm not.*
> *I'm the white buzzing sound. The*
> *terrible white light men make.*
> *Their machine that hates me.*

I remember nothing. Nothing.
And I smile at nothing.
They think I'm better.
I remember nothing.
Nothing.
I long for the comfort
of darkness, the long
black tunnel where the light
of memory flickers at the end. . . .
The white buzzing sound wipes me empty.

❖

"I feel a lot better talking to you and all. Clara's lucky to have a mom she can talk to and all." Annie twisted her full skirt in her fingers.

The ride to her house through meadows, past old farm houses and fields left me relaxed at the end of a warm, beautiful day. I smiled at Annie.

"Would you come in and see my room, some of the stuff my grandfather's given me?" Annie's eyes were expectant like a child's.

However, I had no desire to meet her father. "I wouldn't want to barge in on your father, Annie. Plus, it looks like he has company." There were a few cars parked in front.

"He won't even notice us, believe me. I come and go pretty much like a ghost or something." Annie laughed. "There's something I want to show you."

I heard laughter on the other side of the house, but we didn't see anyone as we walked to her room. Her room was beautiful. Old lace hung on the windows and a large piece of thickly knit lace covered a deep pink quilt on her bed. Antique dolls perched on shelves and her dressing table was filled with beautifully made perfume bottles.

"A lot of them just hold water. I just like to look at them. This is what I wanted you to see." Annie handed me the most stunning Japanese kimono I'd ever seen. It was a deep emerald green, silk, and on both sides the most delicate flowers, pink and yellow chrysanthemums, grew from the hem, where a row of pale scallops were perfectly woven, to the shoulders.

"Do you have company?" Annie's father stood in the doorway. He smiled at me with his full boyish charm. He had a beard, a hand-woven shirt from some Latin American country, and the usual country shoes, which I refuse to wear: Birkenstocks. They depress me with their air of stamp-of-approval. You buy them and automatically join a club.

I sighed. "I'm Clara's mother, Lupe, and I drove Annie back."

"I see. Yes, Clara. Glad to meet you. Hope it didn't inconvenience you too much."

Before I could answer he continued: "You know, Annie, if I don't drive you, it's best to stay home. You know I can't always drive you everywhere you want to go."

"You never drive me. I'd always be home if I waited for you to drive me."

"She hitchhikes without my permission, you see. . . ."

"That's why I want a car. . . ."

"Maybe, just maybe, when you're eighteen." He dismissed Annie and focused on me. "Would you like to join us for some wine in back?"

"If I don't have a car and you don't drive me, Dad, I'm going to keep hitchhiking. . . ."

I wanted to tell him about the near-rape incident, but the panic in Annie's eyes stopped me.

"She always gets hysterical, just like her mother. When she shows me her nonhysterical, rational side I'll consider the car. Teenage girls, spare me. . . ."

"I'm teaching Clara to drive. It'll take some of the transportation pressure off me, especially out here in the boonies. Annie appears as *rational*," I added emphasis here, "as Clara. I sure wouldn't want Clara hitchhiking." I could see he was beginning to get angry.

"I forgot to introduce myself. I'm Don. If Annie needs a ride home again, please have her call me. It was very nice meeting you." He turned to leave.

"Hysterical like my mother? You mean, crazy like my mother, don't you? After you got through with her she's never even driven a car!" Annie's face was red, with tears falling fast.

He glanced at me and said, "See what I mean? Hysterical. I apologize for her behavior."

"You mean misdiagnosis, don't you?" I found myself saying.

"I suppose we're all entitled to our own opinions." He smiled stiffly and strode away, his Birkenstocks smacking the wooden floor flatfootedly. I thought of Donald Duck to relieve my own tension. I turned to smile at Annie, to touch her shoulder.

94

She fell into my arms saying, "He got her so many shock treatments, that bastard, that the last time I saw her she didn't even know who I was." Annie sobbed, leaning into me. "She kept saying something that I couldn't understand. She was almost whispering to herself, and when I got close to her to hear if I could understand, she'd stop talking. That's what he did to her. . . ."

"When did you last see her?"

"About six years ago?"

"Maybe she's better."

"She's institutionalized. She's gotten worse. That's what they say." Annie pulled away from me, grabbing some tissue from her dressing table and wiping her face. "Maybe I am hysterical. Maybe I am just like my mother. Look at me, right?"

"You're not hysterical, Annie, you're in pain. . . . Annie, what's your truth? Think about it. What's your very own truth?"

Annie started to smile. "The truth is, I got you in here to give you that kimono. Don't say no, 'cause I really mean it. I want you to have it and all. I felt real good driving over here. Our talk and all."

"I can't take this, it's way too much. . . ."

"Okay, then borrow it. I'll take it back later. I have a few more, so I won't even miss it. Isn't it a beautiful kimono, that emerald green, it reminds you of queens and empresses, doesn't it? It belonged to my mother and all, only she hated the shells at the bottom. She hated the ocean. I guess she was afraid of drowning 'cause she couldn't swim and all." Annie paused, remembering, as sadness took her smile. She whispered, "She used to write poetry sometimes. You know, there was one word I caught. You know, it sounded like *empty*."

"Maybe that was her truth."

"It didn't save her."

"Maybe it did."

"Would you put the kimono on for a minute?" Annie smiled shyly. "Can you swim?"

I smiled back at her as I put on the kimono. "I'm a very strong swimmer. I love the ocean." I ran my hands over the luxurious silk and looked down at the pale scallops at the hem. From this angle the lush pink and yellow flowers seemed to spiral from the bottom of an emerald sea, from the pale, lucid scallops, toward me. It was rushing toward me, this invitation to growth, and I imagined I felt *her* vertigo when she'd worn it. But it passed quickly.

Annie listened to Clara's mother drive away. Music was playing in back and the aroma of barbecue was beginning to make her hungry. She couldn't picture her mother's face, no matter how hard she tried. She picked up her favorite doll, cradling it against her.

"The white buzzing sound wipes me empty, but I love you, Annie. Empty Annie."

❖ Her Spiral Shell

I hear my mother crying, "We can wait another year, she's small for a ten-year-old, you can see that, she might die from the shock . . ."

"How old were you, remember? And you didn't have a doctor, our mother's sisters, our own mother, did it for you. The doctor's going to anesthetize her. She'll feel nothing," my mother's sister answers her with growing impatience.

"We felt everything, I remember. Remember how we lost consciousness from the pain? But she'll feel nothing with the medicine. She has you to thank," my mother's other sister says in a gentle voice.

"She'll be ready next year . . ."

"Next year she may be a woman and too late. He'll never forgive you for that, you know that. As it is, he feels a doctor is unnecessary, but he does it for *you*." There's jealousy in my aunt's voice. Everyone knows my father loves my mother unnaturally. I've heard my aunts say he's made sure she has only two children, my brother and I, so that she'll always be young and beautiful, not old and tired like they are with so many children, all of them.

"Is the doctor ready? Let me help carry her," my mother says. She's crying. The other night when she supervised my bathing, she told the girl to go. She spoke to me softly, stroking my long, wet hair: "We could run away, you and I, I have money, enough to get away, but I don't know where we'd go, little one, I don't know where we'd go . . ." She began to cry and I cried with her because I didn't know where to go either.

A friend who had it done to her says it's like being cut by fire and that her mother told her having children would be nothing after that. I wonder, if it's unnecessary skin, why are we born with it? Sometimes when I touch it, though I'd be horribly punished if they knew, it feels like something wonderful might happen, just for a minute.

I feel my mother's large, soft breasts cradling my head; my aunts carry my legs. I look up at my mother and smile. I love her, the way she smells, the way she feels.

"She's awake . . ."

"All she had was warm wine, of course she's awake. The doctor's waiting to anesthetize her."

I don't know what the long word means, but it frightens me. My mother said I'd feel nothing, that I wouldn't feel cut by fire, that the doctor will make the pain sleep. I don't want to be cut by fire, I don't want to be cut by fire, I don't want to . . . I grab my mother, beginning to weep, I see she's crying openly. I think her thoughts: The fire, the fire beyond screaming . . .

"She's too small, you can see that, you can see that!"

Now I'm terrified. I only want my mother. I only want my mother. I only want my mother, if it's unnecessary skin why was I born with it, don't touch me, don't touch, why is it evil, why would it make me bad, why is it evil . . .

"Leave her to us, the doctor is getting impatient! He shouldn't even be here for this! Let go of her!"

"She's right, leave her to us, it'll be nothing, the doctor is waiting to kill the pain, she'll feel nothing."

I cling to my mother. I begin to scream, but they take me from her. My mother's beautiful face is unhappy, full of pain. They take me from her soft, full breasts, but she presses something into my hand. Her spiral shell. The one she carries everywhere. She told me a secret once: "Even if they take the skin, there's a secret place, like this shell, where, if your husband loves you, you will feel his love."

The doctor is angry. "Cover her mouth. I have no time for this foolishness. Who ever heard of anesthesia for this procedure?"

One of my aunts, her eyes glitter with unconcealed victory, the other feels pity, but they both hold me down, covering my mouth with a folded towel or I'd devour them whole, as the fire, the fire, the leaping, scraping, angry fire between my legs devours me.

A Prostitute Compassionate Am I ❖

Francie'd had the fresh beauty of a girl when she'd blossomed at eleven. It had lasted for a year, until her grandfather raped her, raping her until he, at last, died. He owned the house they lived in, the money they were to inherit after his death, so no one believed Francie when she tried to tell her mother, then her father. He'd raped her surrounded by her dolls, and though they, the dolls, believed her, there was nothing they could do. Finally, she'd taken her beloved dolls to a patch of soft, turned earth where the bulbs would go, and buried her dolls deeper than the bulbs would be planted, and waited for the old man to die.

Now, at thirty-two, Francie is no longer fresh or beautiful, but there is something unmistakably beautiful about her. If you saw her in a restaurant, eating and talking, you'd probably notice it, but wouldn't be able to pinpoint it: the quality of absolute acceptance.

I became her friend by accident, one night, when I went dancing alone after a fight with my lover. I felt excited and brave, imagining myself choosing an anonymous lover for one night among the many single men surrounding me. Only when the first man asked me to dance, I was stunned by his obvious stupidity. The second man was a half notch better, complaining in the mentality of a toddler about his ex-wife. How I pitied her. When he came back to ask me to dance, I leaped to my feet and began dancing by myself, pretending to be in a state of untouchable ecstasy. That's when Francie joined me, dancing with upraised arms and smiling the ecstatic smile I was pretending to smile.

Francie was wearing a kind of belly dancer's outfit with layers of various colored veils wrapped and loosely waving around a bare-shouldered, low-cut, silky dress. She wore a four-stranded belt of small, white seashells; it moved seductively on her hips as she danced. On her arms she wore bunches of bracelets, so when she lifted her arms to the music, she made some of her own. We were dancing to rock and roll, but watching Francie I felt transported to ancient Egypt or Greece. Babylonia.

"Do you mind if I sit with you?" Francie asked, sitting down. "All the tables are taken." She smiled at me.

"Sure, I'm by myself tonight. Are you a dancer? You look like a belly dancer, your arm movements and all." I smiled back. "I love your outfit, all those veils, and that belt is really something."

Francie laughed a low, private laugh. "Thank you. I got this belt on a journey to Africa a few years ago."

The cocktail waitress came, and Francie asked me if I'd like to share a carafe of white wine. I agreed.

"Are you a dancer?" I asked again.

Francie smiled to herself as she stretched her legs, moving her head to the music. "I dance, but I'm not a dancer, professionally that is. I'm a sex worker." She saw my confusion and repeated her words to me, looking directly into my eyes. "I'm a sex worker."

"Do you mean a sex therapist?" My mind took a couple of leaps, but I couldn't quite make it to a clear spot.

Francie smiled only in her eyes: compassionate, calm, fearless. Then she said, "A prostitute compassionate am I."

My mind finally landed as I remembered one of my favorite books. "I read that in WOMAN'S MYSTERIES, Esther Harding. That's Ishtar speaking, the Goddess. Are you saying you're a prostitute?" I returned her steady gaze, sensing her challenge. If I looked away, that would be it. Respect was important to this woman. I felt her intelligence probe mine like a laser.

"Yes, I'm a prostitute."

Our wine arrived and I poured. "In the ancient Goddess religions there were temple priestesses who gave themselves sexually." It was hard to talk over the music.

"I know. I've read that book and some others. In fact, just regular women fucked a stranger, at least once in the temple, making them virgin, in the Goddess sense. Spiritually." Francie took a quick sip of her wine and jumped to her feet. She twirled to the music, her shell belt following her hips like obedient snakes. Her red hair was piled on her head. I imagined it down, past her shoulders and strange men touching it. I wanted to feel sorry for her, but she didn't look beaten. I shivered, feeling, suddenly, so alone, like an unloved child.

I took two large gulps of wine and made myself get up and dance. Francie was on the other side of the room, so I faced the band and danced. Something in me unleashed itself and, finally, I moved with real abandon. When I looked to my left a young dark-haired man smiled at me. He appeared to be following my dance steps, my rhythm, but then it struck me—maybe they're his own. His eyes were intelligent. Then the band began a slow dance. As I started to walk away, he grabbed my hand, and when I turned to face him he was smiling as though to say, You know me.

His body felt exactly the right blend of musculature and softness. It was hard to tell who was leading who. We looked at each other and laughed.

If I'd had children in my teens, he could've been my son. Another of the Goddess's idiosyncrasies: son and lover. I, however, had no children. I taught English, wrote poetry periodically, almost always had a lover—always my age or older. I glanced over at my table, and Francie smiled at my situation.

"Are you a student?" I asked him, dreading he'd say he went to the university where I taught. I'd never had an affair with a student, though it was a matter of personal pride with most of my male colleagues, the bastards. One of my women students had confided in me that another student had invited her to join one of Miller's orgies. Unbelievable. Or maybe I was a prude.

He tightened his hold on my waist. I noticed his mouth was full, feminine. "No, I'm an actor. I'm visiting from Southern California. And you?"

"I teach and write a little."

"What do you write?"

"Poetry."

"A poetess, how sexy."

I went back to sit with Francie, and he disappeared to the bar. He made me promise to dance when the band came back. The club piped in some quieter music, making it possible to speak without shouting.

"Should I do it?" I asked her, though I already knew I would.

"Of course you should. Even I wouldn't charge that one. He's definitely good luck, a gift from the Goddess." She laughed deep in her throat.

"So, then, sometimes you don't charge?" I felt like a little girl asking a sex question.

"There are certain services I charge more for, like head jobs, with AIDS and all. I don't swallow. My grandfather used to make me swallow. I didn't even know what it was." Francie looked up at the darkened stage.

"Your grandfather did that to you . . ."

Francie pulled out a small silver pipe from her purse and pressed some leaves into it. "Do you smoke? This is mellow stuff."

"Is it okay here?" I looked around.

"I do it all the time." For a moment she looked like a little girl, hunched over, doing a secret thing as she lit it. She passed it to me. I felt innocent somehow, bringing the sweet smoke into my lungs. The cocktail waitress came to see if we wanted more wine and saw the pipe. "Can I have a drag?" She squatted and smoked. It was turning into the Bad Girls Club.

When the cocktail waitress was gone, Francie said, "I don't charge when they're a gift from the Goddess, like your friend, or a gift to the Goddess." She pressed more leaf into the small silver pipe and lit it.

"What do you mean a gift to the Goddess?"

"There's one guy who told me he was molesting his little girl. I asked him if he'd raped her and he said no, but he thought he was going to sooner or later. So I told him he could come to me for free, but he had to promise to stop molesting her."

"How do you know he keeps his promise?"

"I see her once or twice a month and we talk. She's ten, almost the age I was when my grandfather started with me." Then Francie told me about her dolls, how she'd buried them in the garden.

The band came back on stage and immediately the room was filled with deafening music. I could see the young man walking toward me, so I said, "Francie, give me your phone number so we can get together. Do you want to?" I pulled out a pen, some paper. She smiled and wrote her number down.

As I got up to dance, Francie stood up. "Here, take this, I have another one just like it." She reached around her hips and unclasped the African shell belt and handed it to me. "Take it, it's good luck. It means you're a woman."

A couple of weeks later, when I went to Francie's place for dinner—she insisted on cooking dinner—when she opened the door I handed her a beautifully made red-headed doll. "Take it," I said, "it's good luck. It means you're a child." I was wearing the African shell belt around a comfortable black dress. I loved the feel of its weight on my hips.

Francie stared at the doll for a moment, then nearly grabbed her out of my hands. Smiling, she wept. "How was he?"

"Wonderful." I wept with her.

❖ The Others

ON THE COAST BY THE SOUTH CHINA SEA

Why are they taking so long? the boy thought, looking up toward the door while keeping his fingers busy with the plastic toy he was assembling. The ones he'd made were placed, carefully, in a row next to him on the bare, dirty floor. He looked at the finished toys and wondered why children would want to play with such ugly things, but the guardian told him to work faster, no talking, because children, smart and rich children, around the world were waiting for these beautiful toys, and the guardian would laugh. Carefully, he looked up at the door where his sister had gone, where she'd been taken to be hurt again, he knew, but the door didn't open. A dull fear ached in his stomach.

Outside, it was raining and a hard wind made the building shudder from time to time. It was absolutely quiet as he and the other children worked. Speaking was punished by the withholding of food or a beating. No food was the worst punishment as they were sometimes fed only once a day. Sometimes, almost as a cruelty, to remind them of comfort, they were given hot tea, or rather hot water with some used tea leaves floating at the top. When this happened, the children would remember their mothers. No matter how hard their lives had been, their mothers or grandmothers had always given them hot tea from time to time. Some of the children would want to weep, some to laugh, when the hot liquid filled their mouths; instead, they chose a wise silence and looked guardedly at each other with secret pleasure.

The children, bent and working in silence, looked like old, tired people, when, in fact, they ranged in age from six to thirteen. The boy who looked toward the door was eight; his sister was twelve. They'd been sold together to this toy factory to work. He remembered his mother's face, so clearly, as she touched his sister's face, then his, and then turned her back as they left with one of the men. She'd packed them some few precious vegetables to eat in strips of cloth and fresh tea leaves, but he took their small packages and ridiculed them when they wept and said they were hungry.

"You don't know what hunger is yet!" He'd pinched his sister's arm, making her cry out. "You're unhealthy, too fat!" the man had laughed.

When they'd taken her in the room before, she'd walked slowly out and sat next to her stack of plastic toys and just stared at them. He'd hissed her name as quietly as possible, and when she'd looked up at him, her eyes were swollen and lost. Then she'd picked up a toy because the guardian swept them with his eyes. That night, as they slept together, she took his hand and placed it on her soft, wet cheek. "They all hurt me," she whispered. He wept with her, without a sound, touching her cheek as gently as possible.

ON THE SOUTH CHINA SEA

They would've reached the island if the demons hadn't found them. They'd gathered rainwater in bowls to drink, and though their tongues were swollen from thirst, the rainwater kept them alive as they watched for the small, brown swell that would soon rise in the distance. That one brown, *still* swell in the constantly moving, undrinkable water. Salt, salt, salt. How she hated it.

Almost all the babies had died. One of the women had hidden her baby's death, pretending to suckle it, so it wouldn't have to be put into the moving saltwater. Then the demons had come, boarded their small boat, and taken her living baby brother from her mother's arms and thrown him into it, and her father had jumped in to save him, and the demons shot him.

And they'd almost reached the island, she knew it. She'd dreamt it one night, the night before the demons came. Now they had her and another young girl.

She waited. The moment the demon, who held her in his grip, his tail between her legs, let her go, she would leap, fly, turn into salt.

ON AN ISLAND BY THE JAVA SEA

"I had a terrible dream, Grandmother."

"Tell me, child."

"I'm ashamed to tell you, Grandmother."

"You must tell me." Grandmother smiled gently.

Outside their neat, thatched dwelling the sun rose after three days of storms, and the air was so clear and fresh little children could barely eat, they were so anxious to fling themselves into the fresh, warm sun and play. Their bare feet curled in delight as their mothers fed the morning fires and their fathers held the babies, sipping hot, sweet tea with delicate white flowers floating towards their fathers' full, gentle lips.

In a soft voice she said, "I dreamt evil men were violating children my age and everywhere there was screaming while the men laughed. Then they were violating me, and it hurt so that I wished to die, Grandmother."

The grandmother sighed, tears streaming down her brown, wrinkled face. "Child, oh, child, you dream a dream of compassion and that is a good dream. To share another's pain is the highest good. You must never be ashamed. There are such evil men, yes, and such evil happens, yes." She held her granddaughter close and stroked her soft, long, black hair in familiar comfort.

"Now eat your food, all of it, and we'll take these blossoms to the Goddess. Each petal is a child's soul and we'll ask the Goddess to give them comfort and restore their innocence."

"That was such a terrible dream, Grandmother. I never want to dream it again." The girl sat up and wiped her eyes with her small, graceful hands. She looked at her grandmother for reassurance and said, "I never want to dream evil again, Grandmother, ever."

The old woman picked up the loose branches filled with white, starry flowers. "Child, if you don't dream the evil, the evil will dream you. If you don't share in the world's pain, the Goddess will not speak to you." She gave a flowering branch to her granddaughter and stood up. "Do you have the shell in your ear to hear her clearly? Come, we must speak to the Goddess, now, while the sun is rising. Do you understand, child?"

"This is my first dream about the others. . . ." The girl's voice was gently resigned, sad and wise, as she and the old woman walked toward the waves, the Goddess, the Java Sea.

❖ Virgin Birth

As Ruby sang the words, "Goin home, goin home, I'm a goin home, quiet like some still day, I'm a goin home . . ." she felt so angry she could cry. It was a terrible urge that came over her every time they sang this "old Negro spiritual" as their friendly, white choir teacher called it, in slightly reverent tones. They were learning it so well their harmonies were beginning to sound like one voice swelling, diverging, then merging from one open mouth. Now, her solo came: "It's not far, just close by, through an open door, work all done, care laid by, going to fear no mo-ore. . . ." Ruby glanced at her teacher and saw that her eyes had tears in them. She wanted to scream, "Fuck this stupid shit!" but instead she lowered her eyes because tears of rage were gathering in them, and the passion of her rage made her innocent, full, fifteen-year-old soprano voice tremble, ever so delicately, making the choir teacher thankful for this young black girl's presence.

Such authenticity, the woman beamed, inwardly, as her tears of compassion streaked her smooth, blemish-free white cheeks. She had hoped one of the black students going to this, almost exclusively white, school would try to join *and* have a voice. "Thank you, Ruby, beautiful."

Ruby looked up at the pretty, young, liberal white teacher—her and her African Peace Corps stories—and it took every ounce of Ruby's will to not scream, "FUCK YOU AND YOUR NEGRO SPIRITUALS!" She veiled her fierceness, a terrible, smoldering presence that swam just beneath the beautifully dressed, African American doctor's daughter who played tennis, skied, spoke French and Spanish and dated white boys; she said, "Thank you."

Instantly, her rage turned into the irresistible urge to vomit. Ruby grabbed her backpack and books and walked, as quickly as possible, to the bathroom.

"My grandmother raised three sets of children and all of them sold before they were fully grown. But she said it was better than nothing, so she gave them all her love and taught them about Jesus who loved everyone, black or white—yes, that's what she couldn't get over, black or white—no matter what they do." Ruby's grandmother would look out the window and sigh. "Had to be the Son of God to do that, my girl, don't you think?"

Ruby would nod, yes.

"My grandmother said some of the children were from her husbands and some from the owner-man. That's how it was then, she said, and she loved all her children just the same. She told me she had a real light-skinned baby girl, and she was sold even sooner than the others to work in a house like a special child-slave. Jesus help her, what they must've done to that child, Jesus."

"What, Grandma?"

"Don't tell your Mama that ah'm tellin you all a this, you hear?" She could lapse into black English from time to time, but mostly she spoke white English, crisp and perfect like a teacher, which she'd been. Now, she was dying from cancer and lay in bed, mostly, taking her medication for the pain and talking to her granddaughter when Ruby sat with her at night for hours.

"I won't, I promise," Ruby said, waiting to hear more about the special child-slave who was light skinned. Ruby was light skinned and, though no overt message was ever conveyed, the unspoken message from her parents was approval.

"My grandmother told me about another woman who had a light-skinned child with blue eyes. He had our hair, but he had the bluest of eyes. Well, she knew the owner-man, the father, would put great value on that child. Do you know what she did?"

Ruby waited, heart pounding.

"I think you're old enough to hear this. I was younger than you when I heard it. Well, child, she killed her blue-eyed baby and plucked out his eyes. She left him on her bed, wrapped in a blanket. He was nearly a year old and she'd suckled him, waiting to choose her time. They would've taken him soon after the weaning like a calf from a cow. That's how it was. My grandmother al-

ways told me this woman was wicked, killing her own little baby, but that sometimes she'd think of her just to keep on going. A woman who could pluck out her own baby's eyes, even if they were blue like his father's. My grandmother would say, shaking her head, 'Have to be the Devil or a God to do a thing like that, oh sweet Jesus. Hard enough to be Gods's Mama and let them kill your chile,' she'd say. What do you think, Ruby?"

"I don't know, Grandma," Ruby managed to whisper. "It's pretty awful, I think." Then it came to her: "But at least she didn't let them get the best of her."

"Or what they thought was the best of her—yes! That's exactly what I think. You can't help but admire that woman."

"Do you think she acted like God?" Ruby cringed from the amazement on her grandmother's face, but she hadn't thought to censor herself.

The old woman laughed long and softly, almost to herself. "I think she acted like a Goddess."

"A Goddess?" Ruby echoed. Her grandmother had always told her African Goddess stories, stories about creation, the beginning of things, but never anything like this. That she killed or would kill her own child.

"Do you want to see the shell?" Her grandmother rarely brought out the small, worn shell. It fit, neatly, in the palm of the hand. Ruby had seen it maybe twice before, so she became quiet and forgot about the terrible Goddess, a woman who would kill her own. . . .

The old woman took a hand-carved wooden box from beside her bed, and from a pouch on her neck extracted a small key. She fit the key into the lock and the lock gave with a bell-like click. There were old letters, dried flowers, treasured jewelry she no longer wore, and the bundle of soft, red flannel cradling the old, intact shell. She removed it and held it in her hands. It was smooth, almost translucent, and conically shaped.

"Would you like to hold it, Ruby?"

"May I?" Ruby gasped. She'd never been allowed to hold the shell.

Her grandmother placed it in the open palm of her hand. It felt so light, so fragile. She was afraid to breathe for a moment.

"Did I ever tell you how your first African grandmother brought this shell with her? Of course I didn't. Your mother asked me not to tell you these stories as I told her. She said it was time to put them behind us, time to go on." The old woman smiled. "Well, I think it's always time to go on, but as long as one of us, daughters of that African woman, remembers, we have to keep telling it. It makes us strong, Ruby, so I'm going to tell you now."

Ruby waited in silence. A shiver of excitement went up her spine.

"She was a child, my grandmother told me, and her mother put this shell into her vagina. And the story goes, she wasn't raped in the crossing. Her mother died and her two brothers were sold. But this African woman survived and we are here now."

"My green eyes and light skin come from a white man, don't they Grandma? They raped her, after all, didn't they?" Ruby began to weep.

"Yes, yes, Ruby, the owner-man lives in us, but we live in him, too. We got the best of him, Ruby, and kept the best in us. The shell is yours now."

"I can't keep it. . . ."

"No, it's yours now, to tell your daughter. It's your turn to remember, to tell your daughters, and your sons, about the woman who plucked out her child's blue eyes, how the shell got here, the African Goddess stories of creation. Do you promise, Ruby?"

Ruby nodded, yes, as she wrapped the shell gently into its soft, red flannel blanket. A shiver of recognition went through her as she realized how the shell came to be in her hands: it had been brought forth from a child's vagina like a virgin birth.

❖

She was relieved to find no one home. Just the cook in the kitchen, a white woman, making dinner. She climbed the stairs to her room as quietly as possible. The cook, a kind woman, always greeted her with a snack.

She passed her grandmother's closed door. It'd been closed since the funeral, but this weekend all of her furniture would be removed and the room repainted. Every trace of her grandmother would disappear, and her grandmother's room would be a guest room again.

She locked her bedroom door behind her. Her stomach grumbled and softly complained its lack of food. She'd vomited until only bile rose, bitter, to her mouth.

She took the hand-carved wooden box out from under her bed and, taking the key from a pouch on her neck, she fit the key into the lock and the lock gave with a bell-like click. She removed the red flannel bundle. She'd read every letter her grandmother had saved, mostly love letters from her husband during absences. She was surprised, even a little shocked, to learn the passion between them: "I miss the warmth of your body, the way you smell, especially *there*, my wife. . . ." She smiled at the thought of her grandmother's youthful body inspiring such passion.

"Goin home, my ass," she muttered.

She took off all of her clothing and inspected herself in the full-length mirror. Her body had rounded by her twelfth year and her breasts were full like a woman's. She removed the shell from the soft, red flannel and let the cloth drop to the rug. Then, she spread her legs, slightly squatting, and placed the conical tip at the entrance to her vagina. She began to, slowly, very slowly, push it in. She imagined the African child, younger than herself, receiving it the first time, and it made her keep pushing, though it hurt a little.

It was in, entirely. She looked at her fingers and smiled. Now she knew why the small, white shell was wrapped in the soft, red flannel.

Karma ❖

It was a clear, beautiful morning on the California coast, slightly north of Santa Cruz. The surfers were out, the wind surfers were out, the sailboats, and the well-tanned, well-travelled, well-kept couple was out, going north to San Francisco to meet friends. They'd just returned from sailing the Mexican coastline, their Spanish improved, their perspectives improved. They were almost perfect and they knew it. They only disagreed about one thing. She wanted a child, just one. He didn't want any: "It'll ruin our lifestyle. Can you imagine sailing with a baby? Be real!"

He dreaded her long silences. It meant she was going to brood again, about the so-called baby. He imagined it cutting teeth, relieving itself on endless disposable diapers, screaming for its food, and waves of revulsion passed over him. His father'd been trapped by his sons' births; it wasn't going to happen to him. Besides, he told himself, that's all the world needs, one more body.

"Put on a Stones tape, would you, honey?"

She stared out the window, listlessly, watching intense, green fields and rows and rows of artichokes, brussels sprouts whiz by. In one field a group of people were bent over working. She saw some children huddled together in the back of an old truck. Though the sun was rising steadily, it hadn't reached the early morning frost yet, glittering on the broad, jagged artichoke leaves.

"Why do you suppose those people have so many kids? Did you see those kids sitting in the back of that old, beat-up truck shivering to death? Probably haven't had breakfast yet. . . ."

"Would you please put the Stones on?"

"I don't feel like hearing the Stones."

"Well, you are tonight, remember?"

"I don't feel like hearing them right now, okay?"

"Put something on, maybe that New Age tape."

She reached for it and clicked it in. Its soothing tones threatened to calm her down, so she thought of the children shivering in the morning cold. She thought of their parents, probably ignorant, illegal aliens, she added with distaste. Why do they have so many children, absolutely stupid.

Another group of brown people hunched over in the fields, but this time she couldn't spot any children. The New Age bells and flute created an eerie peace between them. Her usual visualization was swimming into her favorite cave in Baja. They'd anchored there for a week. The cave was small with ledges for sitting. She'd swim in, alone, with her usual thrill of terror, imagining Cave Monsters waiting in the far back where she couldn't go. Then, sitting on the ledge, adjusting her eyes, she'd listen to the slow hiss of the sea and dripping water all around her. Once, with secret pleasure, she swam into the cave clutching a favorite shell she'd found. On a piece of tape she'd written ETHAN OR MELISSA in black waterproof ink. She'd placed it on the ledge beside her and said their names in time to the dripping water. She'd wept, but in the cave everything was wet anyway. That night she was aggressive and passionate, and he congratulated himself on his masculinity, his good sense for bringing her here; swimming was so good for her.

"The children in Baja looked pretty happy. People seemed to just eat from the sea. Why do you suppose those people come here to pick vegetables and live in shacks?" She saw his face, smooth with the music, tighten with anger.

"Do you realize if those people didn't pick those vegetables—if the farmers, the owners that is, had to hire union help—we'd be paying about two dollars for a bunch of broccoli, one-fifty for lettuce, two for a pound of tomatoes, maybe more. Grow up, Lisa, that's life."

Her throat tightened with an unnameable anguish. "What about those children freezing in a truck, what about their breakfast, what if they don't go to school. . . ."

"Lisa, that's not our problem. I'm not God or the president of the United States and neither are you. Do you want to pay two dollars for a bunch of broccoli?"

Tears stung her eyes. Usually, she'd agree or she'd cry, and he'd comfort her with wise superiority. What did she know, stupid little girl. *I'm* the child in this relationship, she thought angrily.

"Yes, I'd pay two dollars a bunch for broccoli, even three dollars a bunch if those people could live like human beings!" Her voice was firm, without a tremor.

His mouth twisted, cynically; he'd been waiting for this. "Then, Lisa, those people wouldn't even be tolerated in this country. They'd ship them out of here quicker than you could say, 'One super burrito, hold the hot sauce.' They're tolerated, in so many numbers, so that we can have broccoli at seventy-nine cents a bunch and artichokes, four for a buck." He felt triumphant; she was speechless.

She felt cold with anger, but clear and calm, as though she'd just faced the Cave Monsters and she were in the peace of the small cave with the pathetic shell: ETHAN OR MELISSA written in black waterproof ink.

"Ron, what if we had children, and we had to go to Mexico with only what we could carry and pick their food so that they could have credit cards and sailboats and come to our country to vacation. . . ."

"You're overexaggerating, as usual. First of all"—she wasn't succumbing to his impeccable logic, so reality it had to be—"we aren't going to have children, remember? So, that's an absurd hypothesis. It's not our karma to live in Mexico and come here and pick food for the citizenry. . . ."

"You mean, even if I got pregnant you wouldn't want it?" The black waterproof ink, ETHAN OR MELISSA, loomed before her eyes, startling her.

"Look, Lisa, I've been meaning to talk to you about this. I plan on getting a vasectomy next month or so. I wouldn't expect you to do it, so I've decided. . . ." The flute rose high and pure, perfect, reminding him of his own near-perfection, as though echoing him, answering him, *Strive for perfection*. ". . . that the karma and the genes end here. I guess that makes me the prototype." He smiled, pleased with himself.

The soft, cave part of her wanted to sob and say, "What about Ethan and Melissa, what about the small, eternal cave dripping water, what about the Cave Monsters in the far back?" Instead, the steel she used only with others, rarely with him, rose in her. There was no music anymore, just the sound of the BMW motor purring with monotonous precision.

116

"Why didn't you ever go in the cave with me?"

"What cave, Lisa?" She caught him by surprise. He'd expected a clinging, weepy exchange and now she was talking about a *cave*.

"You know, the one in Baja, where we anchored."

"I prefer not to, that's all. . . ."

"You know, the other day I read in the paper that the farmworkers group, the one headed by that Chávez guy, is protesting the use of insecticides on the crops. The people who work the fields are getting cancer and birth defects, and he claims we're eating it—you know, the seventy-nine-cents-a-bunch broccoli is full of insecticides, good stuff like that." She thought of the shell with the tape stuck onto it; she hoped the tape had soaked off. She hoped the Cave Monsters had eaten it. She laughed, suddenly, and clicked the Stones into the tape player. . . . " Paint it black, paint it black, you devil," a woman screamed.

He wanted to hit her. How dare she, the stupid bitch, best him? He wanted to say, "We'll buy only organic from now on," but she was snapping her fingers to the Stones.

She put the window down, letting the chill air into the warm car. "Maybe you are the prototype, after all, Ron!" She started to laugh in long peals of hilarity, letting the wind whip her hair, bringing tears to her eyes.

People of the Dog ✥

(To the children of Mexico City)

The young man, with the wind god clinging to his back, runs ahead of me. His entire body is tattooed with snakes, birds, and circles. They are strangely wonderful. Beautiful. They crawl, fly, and spin up his powerful legs, to his groin, to his chest and back, and the wind god is strapped to his back like a baby. Is he his mother, I wonder, chasing him, knowing I will never catch him. I laugh, thinking of how a wind god would be born from a man: a fart. Why would a god want to be a baby? Why does he choose the young man with the beautiful tattoos? Maybe he's safer with a man, I think. Women are weak. My mother was weak. She could no longer feed me, protect me from the new man who fed us all. When he took my food, she cried. When he hit me with his fists till I bled, she cried. When he threatened to kill me, she cried. Go to the city, you'll survive there, my mother said, so I came. I'm almost a man, I'm almost ten. I sleep with four other boys, two younger. The older boys torment us, raped the youngest, made him whimper all night, now he's shy and will not speak.

The young man, with the wind god clinging to his back, climbs into a boat and, kneeling, begins to paddle. I feel the water at my feet and smile at the freshness. I haven't bathed since my mother's house. The baby wind god smiles at me, upside down, his head thrown back. It must be uncomfortable and stupid to be a baby and have someone take you wherever they want to go, however they want to take you. But the wind god does look happy, like he trusts the young man, like he wants him to be his mother and carry him everywhere, so I jump into a boat and begin to paddle, following the smile of the baby wind god. The young man never looks at me, as though he doesn't even know I'm chasing him. Just the baby wind god knows I'm chasing him. I paddle so hard and fast, changing sides of the boat to make me go straight, that I'm covered with the sweet lake water. I'm not tired at all. If I was ever hungry, I don't remember. If I was ever thirsty, I don't remember. If I was ever hurt, I don't remember. If I was ever afraid, I don't remember. The young man's tattoos begin to crawl, fly, and spin faster and faster, his skin seems to be dancing and the baby wind god looks at me and laughs. A fart, a fart, he says in baby talk, but all I smell is the sweet lake water. If I was ever afraid, I don't remember.

The young man, with the wind god clinging to his back, glides under a half-circle rainbow, and when I follow him I'm covered with all the colors, only I have no tattoos, but it's better to be lots of colors than just naked with nothing on. His snakes, birds, and circles dance with color, but the baby wind god, even though he has hands and feet and a head, is beginning to look like a cloud. When he opens his mouth, a small, jagged piece of lightning shoots out and drops into the water. It sizzles and turns into a glowing shell. I grab it and put it into my mouth, it tastes like light, I laugh out loud. If I ever felt pain, I don't remember.

The young man, with his wind god clinging to his back, raises the paddle over his head and yells with joy like a song. There's land and a beautiful city. There are strong and fearless Indians everywhere and their women smile, bathing their children and washing their own long, black hair in the morning sun without fear or shame. They look at the young man—his dancing snakes of red and purple, his birds of blue and green, his spinning circles of yellow and orange—and lower their eyes with respect. I look at the beautiful city and it feels familiar, like Mexico City, when I first saw it, before I entered it, before it ate me up. But this city feels like a long time ago when there were Indians everywhere, people that looked like me and my mother, not the Mexican who wants to kill me. I look at the baby wind god and ask, Is this Mexico City long ago? The baby wind god opens his mouth and an eagle flies out and lands on a cactus, stretching his huge wings and turns his head from side to side and shits. I want to laugh, but the young man turns, for the first time, and looks at me. Only his face is naked, except for one small tattoo on his forehead that looks like the moon or sun. Sometimes it's the moon, sometimes it's the sun. One side of his face is gentle, the other side is fierce. He turns away from me and steps onto the shore. The young man holds his fingers in a circle, his hand high in the air. There are drums beating and the sounds of women crying, as though someone's died. The men gash their arms and legs so that blood runs out. The cactus that the eagle rests on blooms, full of soft, feathery flowers, and a snake sleeps under the cactus in the warm sun. The snakes and birds on the young man's body are still, and so are the circles. He looks like stone. Then the baby wind god becomes a thin, white cloud and passes through the young man's circled fingers. The thin, white cloud comes to me and I breathe him in. If I am dead, I don't remember. Quickly, I leap from my boat and I know what I must do. I leap and cling onto Quetzalcoatl's back and I remember peace, a clear, wide peace as big as the sky, as far as I can see and even farther. Now I know we will go together to look for her, she who isn't weak, she who feeds and protects us. I will remember Quetzalcoatl, I will remember the wind god clinging to his back, I will remember the baby wind god.

I will remember birth.

The woman bends over the child's body, pushing his thick, black hair from his forehead. The blankets that cover him are filthy. She notes that his shoes are still on, stuffed with rags against the cold. A tube of glue lies next to him, uncapped. There is no sign of blood, no sign of struggle. His face looks innocent, terrible with peace and the stillness of death. His face is without pain and she imagines a kind of light surrounding him, but she straightens herself immediately. The woman is Mexican, but the Indian in her blood has claimed her features.

The boy who'd come to her office was one of the boys they fed and clothed when they came to the shelter, when the funds were there. He'd asked her to come with him because his friend wouldn't wake up. He said his friend had gone with a man and he'd paid his friend with money and some pills. He tells her a younger boy is missing and that he thinks the older boys have killed him.

Sometimes, the woman sighs, I think the dead ones are better off than the living. The sigh is a mixture of sadness and anger. There are no parents to contact, no relatives, no one to mourn this child, and the next one and the next. Now, I'll go call the police, and they'll come and take the body and dispose of it like a dog.

The woman doesn't know that the ancient one, Quetzalcoatl, came from a clan called the Chichimecs. People of the Dog.

The boy quickly probes the dead boy's pockets and takes the remaining pesos. The woman sees it but says nothing. Like a dog, she thinks, covering the dead boy's face with the filthy blanket. The seven-month fetus within her moves, with a leap, making her sigh loudly, disturbing the room with her sudden wind.

The Empress of Japan ❖

Dovey pulled the mail out with her free hand as she leaned on the cane with her other one. Both hands were twisted with arthritis. She'd ceased to condemn them ugly whenever she took the time to examine them. After she'd fallen on the front porch steps leading up to the small, patiently rotting cottage and broken her right wrist catching herself, she'd come to a peace with her hands. As the wrist and hand healed she'd sympathized with both hands: she'd brought up five children with her hands, hand washing everything most of her life and sewing and darning every hole and ironing and cooking every single meal in their lives, except for the time she'd had pneumonia. With her hands she had run the post office and sold cold beer, sandwiches, and such to the travellers and locals on the stretch of road beyond the small walkway in front of her cottage that led most of them to Reno. Circus Circus or whatever they jabbered about, Dovey thought as she leaned onto her sturdy mailbox, dug into the ground by her younger son on his last visit. Circus Circus, like they got to say it twice in case you didn't hear it the first damned time.

"Lord, do have mercy," she muttered, squinting at the one o'clock sun warming the first real spring days after the Ice Age, as she always called winter in the mountains. She squinted her eyes upward, receiving the sun with intense pleasure, until her eyes disappeared entirely into the tough, brown wrinkles of her childlike face.

She'd never really been what some might call pretty or graceful or anything like that. Well, maybe in her teens, maybe—but she'd cultivated her humor. Not only for others' sakes, but for her own. Five kids, the husband gone one night and never dropping a postcard. Not even once. Dovey came to believe he was dead after the worried, angry spot in her heart became quiet, suddenly, and then he came back one night in a dream the way she'd first seen him when she was fourteen. So, he'd come back, sixteen and full of his old confidence, and that's what she remembered and retained of him, and it had comforted her.

Her swollen legs were getting tired. She poked at the thin, green shoots just beginning to peek through the dirt near the post hole her son had dug for the mailbox. "The dinosaurs are gone now, so come on up and meet the goddamned sun!" Dovey yelled to the daffodils. "Maybe I even have another year or two left in me." Dovey lowered her voice. "Could be I'm the dinosaur hanging on despite all evidence of extinction." She giggled, sounding vaguely like a crow trying to clear its throat.

Now she started back to the cottage, slowly, keeping her eyes on the smooth, stone path, remembering the science books the children had brought home and how interested she'd been reading them. "Pay attention," she'd told them. "Years from now you'll wish you had. If you don't it's like water through a colander." Then she'd grill them worse than their teacher, forcing them to learn what she wanted to learn. About the Ice Age, volcanoes, land masses drifting, the human migration when everything connected. And a lot more, like ocean life—she was amazed to find that the highest mountains were actually in the sea, measuring bottom to top, and that whales were mammals, like herself, giving milk to their young, and that the shark was the oldest life swimming around in the sea, and that dolphins were maybe even smarter than people, and that butterflies went through eight generations on a migration. Dovey had dropped out of school in the sixth grade to work in the cannery and in the fields, but she'd learned to read. It was always one of her secret pleasures, reading after the kids were asleep.

She paused in the spring sun and wondered which generation the monarchs were in as they made their way slowly back to her mountains. She looked out toward the tallest peaks and imagined their fragile, orange-splashed wings working, working so hard just to arrive.

"It damn well makes you think," Dovey muttered softly as she continued to walk, then stopped at the stairs, taking them one at a time like a child just beginning to walk. The phone began to ring. "Oh, hell, well, let it ring, just don't break your friggin neck, old girl." Old dinosaur, she added in her own mind, and she laughed out loud, sounding like a couple of crows trying to clear their throats.

All the heaters were on, but the house was still slightly cold, so Dovey took her thick outdoor gloves off and put her kid's mittens on, as she called them. She poured herself a glass of brandy, taking little sips. "This is my medicine, pure and simple," she told herself, sighing in deep satisfaction. It warmed her and made her remember her children and her own mother much more clearly. Her mother'd been Mexican and her father Scottish. First she'd been called Paloma, but her father hated pronouncing it and they'd changed it to Dovey, though her mother, in private, had always called her "Mi Paloma."

"Mi Paloma, Mamá," Dovey said out loud with a little girl's smile edging her dry lips. "Corazón de mi corazón." Her eyes watered, but it was hard to tell if it was from sorrow or just the cold. Or both.

"No, Daddy didn't want any foreign language in the house, only good ol American, the no-good bastard." He'd left when Dovey was thirteen, the summer her younger sister had been raped and killed. They'd found her body in the fields grown high with hay. Dovey often wondered if her father had done it, but only secretly. No, she'd never said it out loud—how he'd put his hard, nasty thing between her legs and how she'd screamed. No, she didn't even think of him anymore, only Mama and the sister who'd grown into the vague, sweet, frozen category of a dark-haired angel with her deep green eyes.

"Ojos del mar," Dovey said, trying to sound like her dead mother.

As she finished her brandy the phone rang. "Well?" she answered it in her hoarse, cranky voice.

"Well, do you want anything from town this week, Dovey?"

"Was that you earlier, Al?"

"Yeah. Your son told me to pester you about this, cause he said you get down to rice is all. Want anything? I'll be comin up your way tomorrow most likely."

She told him bread, some margarine, including another Christian Brothers brandy, and adding eggs, bacon, some frozen meals to make it look official. He was nice enough, bringing his two kids with him usually. They lived just down the way. "Cookies," Dovey added. "Bring some cookies. Let the kids pick them out and make that a good-sized brandy."

Al laughed loudly. "Only if you share a little with me, Dovey."

"See what I can do, young man." Al was in his forties, younger than her youngest son. The one who was still alive. The other two were dead. The two middle sons.

Dovey leaned back into the comfortable chair and decided to start a fire in the wood stove and have another brandy. She had to concentrate to build a fire or the kindling went to waste and it made her furious. She used to be so good at fires, coaxing one all day and into the night. "Can't even gather my own goddamned kindling," Dovey muttered, twisting newspaper slowly.

The sun was bright through the front room windows, but it was still so far away, and the old pine trees that surrounded the cottage, which kept her cool in the summer, kept her cold in the winter and spring. The paper caught, then the carefully placed kindling, and then the large pieces of wood began their dance with the flame. Dovey sipped her brandy. Her last brandy of the day, till seven or so, when sleep overtook her and then the dreams would come. She didn't fear the notion of death, but she did fear her dreams. Sometimes it was as though she had to find her way back, again and again, to the same tired old body. With death, she told herself, all that's out of the way. "Settled," Dovey said out loud.

The sound of the fire popping and crackling soothed her like the presence of an old friend. She reached for her mail, looking for her daughter's handwriting. Nothing. Mostly junk mail, a card from the senior citizens' club saying they missed her. "Damned liars," she said, smiling. A form letter from some politician and some mail from something called Greenpeace. Dovey had heard nothing from her older son in over ten years. Just like his father, she repeated the familiar judgment to herself inwardly. And her daughter rarely wrote, but she came about twice a year, her three kids grown now, but she was so uncomfortable, angry even. Anyone could tell she just wanted to leave. And the two middle sons dead in some senseless war. "Not a real war, anyway," Dovey said, remembering, and then she said their names out loud but it didn't help. It never helped.

She couldn't remember what they'd looked like as young men, but she could remember them vividly as babies and then boys. Their father had spanked them all too hard—hardening them, she thought. Hardening them and I did nothing, really. How could I?

"¡Mierda!" She spit the word into the thick, afternoon rainbow dust floating in the air all around her. She added two more small oak logs and they caught. Dovey picked up the envelope with the word Greenpeace on it and fingered it.

"Green's a peaceful color like new grass." She remembered the night her daughter's cries woke her up, and she'd gone to her, finding her husband looking sheepish by the side of her daughter's bed.

"Havin a nightmare's all," he'd said.

"I've got to talk to you now," she'd said, her face flushed with fury. Once they'd shut the bedroom door behind them, she continued. "My daddy hurt me and I won't have you hurting her. No!" The words had flown out of her mouth and she'd cowered, instinctively, as his face grew red and his eyes bulged from their sockets. He'd hit the wall with his fist, putting a huge hole in it, and left. There were times she missed him like a presence, but he'd turned ugly, hitting her whenever he'd gotten the chance, and his checks as a laborer were unpredictable, so finally she'd cursed his absence as good riddance.

They'd lived in Sacramento then. When they moved to the old post office house, in the mountains, on the road to Reno, the oldest boy was about fourteen, and it was like a vacation at first.

The girl and I never talked about it after that, Dovey thought, remembering her own mother and how no one had stopped her father from hurting her, or her baby sister. He'd put the pillow over her head, almost suffocating her. Later it was wet with snot and tears and like her private times, when her blood stained everything, she'd wash everything in secret.

Dovey picked up the senior citizen's card and decided to go in maybe next week. She could still drive, but only in daytime. "Lunch and bingo and the rest of the old coots," she said, laughing out loud, amused at herself. In truth, she hated bingo, but no one liked to play Monopoly, her favorite game. "Go and see the old dinosaurs. See who survived the damned Ice Age this year. Maybe even pick up a new oil tablecloth, but that's more than enough to do. Well, if I can't press my damned toe to the gas pedal may as well pack it in. Bury me in back by the chicken coop, grow some damned tomatoes, maybe, from this old carcass." Dovey laughed shortly. "¡Mierda!" she yelled.

The fire exploded in the wood stove as though in response. Dovey smiled at this. She finally felt warm, warm in her bones. "A body needs a fire, a wood fire, to keep warm, and it smells so damned good, so friggin good."

Dovey opened the Greenpeace envelope, turning the lamps on by her chair and read. She could read without glasses and she was proud of it. It was a letter talking about ocean life and about wanting to save it and could she contribute some money. They also, the letter said, demonstrated against nuclear weapons and they showed a picture of a little boat floating next to a huge nuclear ship. There was a man in the little boat. "A Greenpeacer gambling with his goddamned life. Bet he likes Monopoly. Want to play?" she asked his picture.

A small postcard fell out. On the front it said, *Prime Minister of Japan* and beneath the imposing name, his address in Tokyo, Japan. On the other side it said, "Dear Prime Minister, I strongly object to the use of high seas driftnets. . . . High seas driftnets cause the unnecessary deaths of thousands of dolphins and sea birds. . . ." It went on a little more and there was a place for her to sign at the bottom.

"What happened to the Emperor? I bet the Emperor—no, no, better yet his wife, the Empress, wouldn't stand for this if she knew. She must know that dolphins are probably smarter than humans." Dovey shook her head, her usual gesture of impatience, and bent down to the woodstove to add a piece of pine. Probably too busy being wealthy and all to know, maybe, she thought with disgust.

"Well, shit! About time she found out what's happening in her own kingdom, I'd say!" Dovey's voice rose in anger.

With an effort she got to her feet. The worst part's getting the dinosaur going, so walk, old girl, she told herself sternly. In the middle of her bed, under the covers, was her baby, named after her mother and her sixth child. "Come on, Juanita, I have to talk to you." She picked the baby up, wrapped in her own soft blanket. She was dressed in fresh baby clothes. Dovey washed them by hand once a week, rotating her two sets of clothing. The clothing had belonged to the real Juanita, who'd lived only eight weeks, and she was the one Dovey remembered best of all. When her grown daughter came to visit, she hid Juanita comfortably away. She and Juanita talked about everything—well, almost everything, and in this way she hadn't turned into an angel like her sister, beyond her reach.

Dovey brought the baby to her chair by the fire and, cradling her in her arms, sat Juanita up a little so her eyes would stay open and gaze into her own with her usual mute, baby's understanding. "What do you think, mi corazón? Should we do it?"

Dovey read the postcard to her in a fairy tale voice, in a patient voice meant only for children. "You didn't grow up so I didn't read you the science books, but dolphins, mi corazón, are smarter than us humans. I was thinking of sending it to the Empress of Japan. The Greenpeacers ought to know that. She's the one to get on their side. And if she don't

127

know anything, how can she stop them from using these driftnets they're jabberin about, right?"

The baby was silent. Dovey's arm shifted, and Juanita closed her eyes. "There, there, go to sleep, Juanita. What do you know about the sorrow of the world, mi corazón?" Dovey signed her name Paloma McPhail and filled in her address, printing it slowly. "What do you know about the joy of the world, you, my daughter's old doll, mi corazón, Juanita." Dovey smiled at the sleeping baby. "Tomorrow I'll take this to the mailbox, put the flag up early. I'm planting tomatoes this year, Juanita, for you and me. I know Al will pitch in. Wish I had some chicken guts, some old fish, to grow them the right way and maybe some corn like we grew in Sacramento. Maize, but you don't remember that, mi niña."

Her mind began to wander, nearly dropping the baby, but she caught her just in time.

"The old coot survived another Ice Age, Juanita, so Mama can't join you yet, so stay and keep me company, mi corazón, why don't you?" Dovey placed the baby down on the floor close to the wood stove's heat and threw in a wedge of pine.

"¡Mierda!" she yelled just for the sheer pleasure of it like she'd heard her mother do from time to time and what sounded like laughter rolled from her throat like a flock of red-winged blackbirds disturbed in their sleep, calling and calling, in the heights of the green-scented eucalyptus trees as they flashed their blood red message on each wing so beautifully.

Dovey placed two stamps on the postcard next to the words AIR MAIL. "It's about time the Empress realized what's happening in her own kingdom. If she can't stop them from hurting the dolphins, who will, Juanita? You tell me, who?"

Then Dovey crossed out the words *Prime Minister* and right over them printed in larger letters THE EMPRESS. It read in full, THE EMPRESS *of Japan*.

"¡Mierda!" she yelled again, laughing loudly, waking the red-winged blackbirds. She knew it was the only way to make them fly.

❖ The Sand Castle

"Have you dressed yet?" their grandmother called. "Once a month in the sun and they must almost be forced," she muttered. "Well, poor things, they've forgotten the warmth of the sun on their little bodies, what it is to play in the sea, yes. . . ." Mrs. Pavloff reached for her protective sun goggles that covered most of her face. It screened all ultraviolet light from the once life-giving sun; now, it, the sun, scorched the Earth, killing whatever it touched. The sea, the continents, had changed. The weather, as they'd called it in the last century, was entirely predictable now: warming.

Mrs. Pavloff slipped on the thick, metallic gloves, listening to her grandchildren squabble and she heard her mother's voice calling her, "Masha, put your bathing suit under your clothes. It's so much easier that way without having to go to the bathhouse first. Hurry! Father's waiting!" She remembered the ride to the sea, the silence when the first shimmers of water became visible. Her father had always been first into the chilly water. "Good for the health!" he'd yell as he dove into it, swimming as far as he could, then back. Then he'd lie exhausted on the sand, stretched to the sun. Such happiness to be warmed by the sun.

Then the picnic. She could hear her mother's voice, "Stay to your knees, Masha! Only to your knees!" To herself: "She'd be a mermaid if I didn't watch," and she'd laugh. Masha would lie belly down, facing the sea and let the last of the waves roll over her. She hadn't even been aware of the sun, only that she'd been warm or, if a cloud covered it, cold. It was always there, the sun: its light, its warmth. But the sea—they travelled to it. So, she'd given all of her attention to the beautiful sea.

She saw her father kneeling next to her, building the sand castle they always built when they went to the sea. Her job was to find seashells, bird feathers, and strips of seaweed to decorate it. How proud she'd felt as she placed her seashells where she chose, where they seemed most beautiful. Only then was the sand castle complete. She heard her father's voice, "The Princess's castle is ready, now, for her Prince! Come and look, Anna! What do you think?" She saw herself beaming with pride, and she heard her mother's laugh. "Fit for a queen, I'd say! Can I live in your castle, too, Masha? Please, Princess Masha?" "Of course, Mother! You can live with me always. . . ." She remembered her mother's laughing face, her auburn hair lit up by the sun, making her look bright and beautiful.

The sun, the sun, the sun. The scientists were saying that with the remedies they were employing now and the remedies begun twenty years ago—they'd stopped all nuclear testing and all manufacturing of ozone-depleting chemicals was banned worldwide—the scientists were saying that the sun, the global problem, would begin to get better. Perhaps for her grandchildren's children. Perhaps they would feel the sun on their unprotected bodies. Perhaps they would feel the delicious warmth of the sun.

All vehicles were solar powered. The populations took buses when they needed transportation and people emerged mainly at night. So, most human activity was conducted after the sun was gone from the sky. Those who emerged during the day wore protective clothing. Everything was built to screen the sun's light. Sometimes she missed the natural light of her childhood streaming through the windows so intensely the urge to just run outside would overtake her. She missed the birds, the wild birds.

But today they were going out, outside in the daytime, when the sun was still in the sky. Masha knew they were squabbling because they hated to dress up to go outside. The clothing, the gloves, the goggles, were uncomfortable and cumbersome. She sighed, tears coming to her eyes. Well, they're coming, Masha decided. They can remove their goggles and gloves on the bus.

The sea was closer now and the bus ride was comfortable within the temperature controlled interior. Those with memories of the sea signed up, bringing grandchildren, children, friends, or just went alone. Masha had taken her grandchildren before, but they'd sat on the sand, listlessly, sifting it through their gloved hands with bored little faces. She'd tried to interest them in the sea with stories of her father swimming in it as far as he could. But they couldn't touch it, so it, the sea, didn't seem real to them. What was it: a mass of undrinkable, hostile water. Hostile like the sun. They'd taken no delight, no pleasure, in their journey to the sea.

But today, yes, today we will build a sand castle. Masha smiled at her secret. She'd packed everything late last night to surprise them at the sea.

Why haven't I thought of it before? Masha asked herself, and then she remembered the dream, months ago, of building a sand castle with her father at the sea. It made her want to weep because she'd forgotten. She'd actually forgotten one of the most joyful times of her girlhood. When the sea was still alive with life.

Today we will build a sand castle.

They trudged on the thick, dense sand toward the hiss of pale blue. Only the older people picked up their step, excited by the smell of salt in the air. Masha's grandchildren knew they'd be here for two hours and then trudge all the way back to the bus. The darkened goggles made the sunlight bearable. They hated this forlorn place where the sun had obviously drained the life out of everything. They were too young to express it, but they felt it as they walked, with bored effort, beside their grandmother.

"We're going to build a sand castle today—what do you think of that?" Masha beamed, squinting to see their faces.

"What's a sand castle?" the boy mumbled.

"You'll see, I'll show you. . . ."

"Is it fun, Grandmama?" the girl smiled, taking her grandmother's hand.

"Yes, it's so much fun. I've brought different sized containers to mold the sand, and, oh, you'll see!"

The boy gave an awkward skip and nearly shouted, "Show us, Grandmama, show us what you mean!"

Masha laughed, sounding almost like a girl. "We're almost there, yes, we're almost there!"

The first circle of sandy shapes was complete, and the children were so excited by what they were building they forgot about their protective gloves.

"Now, we'll put a pile of wet sand in the middle and build it up with our hands and then we'll do another circle, yes, children?"

The children rushed back and forth from the tide line carrying the dark, wet sand. They only had an hour left. Their eyes, beneath the goggles, darted with excitement.

"Just don't get your gloves in the water, a little wet sand won't hurt, don't worry, children. When I was a girl there were so many birds at the sea we'd scare them off because they'd try to steal our food. Seagulls, they were, big white birds that liked to scream at the sea, they sounded like eagles to me. . . ."

"You used to eat at the sea, Grandmama?" the girl asked incredulously.

"We used to call them picnics. . . ."

"What are eagles, Grandmama?" the boy wanted to know, shaping the dark sand with his gloved hands.

"They used to be one of the largest, most beautiful wild birds in the world. My grandfather pointed them out to me once. . . ." Until that moment, she'd forgotten that memory of nearly sixty years ago. They'd gone on a train, then a bus, to the village where he'd been born. She remembered her grandfather looking up toward a shrill, piercing cry that seemed to come from the sky. She'd seen the tears in her grandfather's eyes and on his cheeks. He'd pointed up to a large, dark flying-thing in the summer blue sky: "That's an eagle, my girl, the spirit of the people."

Sadness overtook Masha, but she refused to acknowledge its presence. The sand castle, Masha told herself sternly—the sand castle is what is important now. "I've brought a wonderful surprise, something to decorate the sand castle with when we're through building it."

"Show us, Grandmama, please?"

"Yes, please, please show us now!"

Masha sighed with a terrible, sudden happiness as she brought out the plastic bag. Quickly, she removed each precious shell from its protective cotton: eight perfect shells from all over the world.

"But Grandmama, these are your *special* shells! You said the sea doesn't make them anymore. . . ."

"It will, Anna, it will." Masha hugged her granddaughter and made her voice brighten with laughter. "Today we will decorate our sand castle with the most beautiful shells in the world, yes!"

✣ The Price of Wonder

Ovo watched the children playing from his Bed of Transformation. He would stay here a few more days and then move to a room of Silence. He loved watching them, imagining his new baby body if he consciously chose to return to the Planet's Physical Existence. "It's such a struggle, always in the beginning, but isn't that the price of wonder?" Ovo asked the children playing below his window.

They moved so quickly, diving into the fresh-water pool, laughing and screaming with delight. Some of the younger ones were being taught to float and swim. "Sun temperature water, I remember," Ovo sighed with pleasure. "Just enough heat to take the edge off the clear, cold water. Look at that little one, barely six months, I imagine." The sound of his own voice soothed him; the voice of this lifetime pleased him. He wished to remember it. A new skill. He'd never done that. If he could do this (and he thought this was important—the voice was rather like one's finger-prints), he might *remember* earlier, next time, if he chose Physical Existence.

The young woman holding the infant looked up, catching Ovo's eyes and smiled, lifting her son out of the water and into the air. The young woman was his great-granddaughter, he realized, laughing, and waved at her. She pointed to herself and then to him, indicating she'd be up to visit. She was barely seventeen with her first child, but she had always wanted to be a Mother and now she was in Training for Motherhood Status One. After a year she would guide a maximum of four children, ages one through four. Adolescents between the ages of twelve and sixteen—those who wished to be Mothers and Fathers—worked with the Mothers and Fathers, two to a cluster. Motherhood and Fatherhood Status Two guided a maximum of four children from five years through eight and so on until the sixteenth year was reached. The age of Vision and Declaration.

Ovo's Healer padded silently into the room. He was dressed in various hues of purple, the color of the Healers, and the material was body temperature tuned, loose fitting, yet tailored to bend, kneel, and move quickly. He was in his early forties and his dark skin still carried traces of those the Ancients called African. In his hands he carried a spray of wild flowers. "Well, I can see you have enough flowers without these," he laughed.

"I think you're right, but let me smell them before you take them away." Ovo bent his face toward the flowers and saw a tiny insect. Carefully, he took it in his hands and held it out to the Healer.

"I thought I'd found them all," he said, taking it. "I'll return in a minute to work with your Energy Centers. You aren't in pain, are you? You aren't masking it—you don't have to. . . ."

"I'm mediating the pain and I feel pleasant, don't worry," Ovo smiled.

The Healer left to put the insect out on a green leaf or the brown earth.

As Ovo stared at the mix of vivid wildflowers, placed in well-made clay pots throughout the room, he remembered, with a comforting flood of memories, his first Vision and Declaration—the Ritual of the Individual Connected to the Whole. Then at twenty-six, thirty-six, forty-six, fifty-six, sixty-six, seventy-six, and two years ago at eighty-six. But his first, his first at sixteen, he remembered the most vividly. . . . All his Mothers and Fathers and his Body/Soul Parents prepared him for four days. He was ritually cleansed and fed only fresh foods. Nothing flesh killed, nothing cooked. The plant-killed and flesh-given foods he thanked with simple poems to the Energy Source. They fed him less and less, until the fourth day he was ready to leave for his Place of Vision and Remembering.

Ovo *remembered* bits and pieces from his many lives through Dreaming and some of those lives, centuries ago, were painful and dark, struggling like an infant toward consciousness and Remembering. He saw himself once as a grown woman and then a grown man, transforming—dying, they'd called it—without joy, struggling for breath, utterly unprepared and fearful. Those dreams woke him up in great pain, tears covering his face.

As Ovo said goodbye to all who had nurtured and guided him, his heart collapsed with fear. He felt suddenly frail and unprotected—What if I can't accept my Remembering and my Vision refused to reveal Itself? Then, I'll be truly alone. An Individual Separated from the Whole. But that doesn't really happen, he'd told himself. The others just continue to nurture and guide you, and you try again in four years and four years after that if necessary. But the pain of separation from the Whole must be experienced alone, as *remembering* must be experienced alone, as Vision must come to you, alone. Ovo saw himself vividly as the sixteen-year-old man longing to take his lover in his arms; with her he wasn't alone in those moments. She had gone to her Place of Vision and Remembering two years before him as she was two years older, but she couldn't speak to him of it, the deep Remembering, because he hadn't gone yet. He still had no Vision.

When she, Sol, gave her Vision and Declaration to the Whole, he'd wept with pride as chills ran up and down his body. How young she was, how ancient she was, how terrifyingly beautiful she was in her fearlessness. Sol. His lover, Beloved, of sixty-three years. He remembered her Declaration, to heal with her music; her Vision had come to her in music. Looking out to the Whole, she'd said, weeping, "I have *remembered* Everything," and they who Knew wept with her. Later, there was music and dance and laughter, the children falling asleep in clusters, carried to their dreams, and those who could, and wished to, danced until the Sun rose in the eastern sky. Dawn, her freshness.

As Ovo forced himself not to clutch her, he held out his fingertips to Sol—she held out hers, just touching his. He felt her energy, sharply, and it was enough. Ovo, at eighty-eight, saw himself turn away from his loved ones and leave toward the rolling, empty hills. Toward the Circle of Oaks. He carried fruit, water, a good blanket, his Life Force Crystal. It was given to him at birth; his Body/Soul mother and father chose it while he gathered his Life Force in the Womb. Then, at four he was allowed to hold it and speak to it for longer and longer periods of time. Then at eight he was allowed to dream with it. Then at twelve his Dreaming began and the bits and pieces of pain, darkness, suffering came to him and he woke sweating, in tears. Everyone had said how wonderful it was he'd begun his Dreaming. But it wasn't wonderful; it had been its opposite: terror.

Ovo saw the Circle of Oaks and he felt the gentle breezes on his thin, young, frightened face—the children played below him and all noise had disappeared. Without realizing it, he'd entered Silence. The Healer returned, and, seeing him, left him alone to his Silence.

The first night he sang to the Oaks, placing his hand on each one, eight in all; but the first night he'd rushed toward sleep in fear. The second

135

night, fear was mixed with a small dose of boredom, but he'd managed to hold fear at bay, ever so slightly, before it overtook him in sleep. Ovo remembered the third night, as Energy coursed through his body, mixed with tinges of the disease that was transforming him, making him leave this familiar body. He saw the Dream and he *remembered*:

Him self killing men.

Him self birthing children.

Him self raping a child.

Him self being raped.

Him self hating his enemy.

Him self loving his enemy.

Him self as absolute darkness.

Him self as absolute light.

Him self cruel, kind, stupid, wise,

unborn, born, transforming, his soul

sustained by an implacable, horrible,

joyous, horrible, wonderful, horrible

l o v e

e n e r g y

mother/father

m y s t e r y

He woke. It was hours before dawn, the freshness. He waited in Silence, making no song. In his body he heard the Silence speak, "In the beginning, always in the beginning, there is Creation where Silence dwells. . . ." Ovo sat, back against a Mother Oak, and saw his Vision in the star-filled night. He saw what he must do. He would tend the Planet and heal through his bounty, what all ate, took into their bodies. He would join the rituals of earth and weather and see the blossoming on the bodies of the Whole. He would safeguard their Body/Soul health. . . . and then he saw himself as a Healer in light purple robes, but he saw himself in old age. The Healers in light purple robes tend the very young, and Ovo had done that in his seventies. Someone else had tended Sol, but he had followed her to the Edge of Transformation until she turned, saying, "Go back, now, love."

The sounds of a baby brought him back from Silence. Ovo looked at his great-granddaughter and her son and smiled. How young she looked, how ancient—how terrifyingly beautiful she was in her fearlessness, this Sol. She held out his great-great-grandson to him, and the child stared at Ovo in wonder mixed with fear. Sol massaged the Energy Centers in his forehead and crown, his temples, the throat, and back up to the crown, visualizing the Light in her great-grandfather's body longing to leave, readying for Transformation.

As Ovo held the baby, he allowed his Vital Energy to merge with the New One. In his body he heard, "In the end, always in the end, there is Creation where Silence dwells. . . ."

Ovo knew his Soul/Spirit would return to the Circle of Oaks where his sixteen-year-old self waited. He saw his great-granddaughter's eyes ask, Will you return?

He wished to answer her because he loved her, but he couldn't. "I will not know until the end begins." Ovo listened to his voice, urging himself to Remember it. The uniqueness of this voice in the Silence.

Sol nodded with understanding. "I brought you this." She handed him a thin, translucent shell from the Waters. They were becoming less rare, but all treasured them.

"A perfect gift. A Being left this shell for further Transformation. Once this held its consciousness. A perfect gift."

The baby stretched and kicked his limbs in sudden excitement as though a wonderful thing had been revealed to him.

El Alma/The Soul, One ❖

Luna parked the car, turned off the lights, put the hand brake on, and rolled down the window a notch. A gust of rain sprayed her face, making her gasp. There was no one on the beach; not one surfer in the water. From this vantage point she could see clear down the beach to a group of rocks where the waves met the cliffs violently. It was soothing to watch the spray leap into the air and disappear: violence to fragility, again and again.

She scratched the palm of her hand, forgetting to stop herself. "Shit," she muttered, "stop scratching." The center of her left palm was getting red and irritated. Probably from the peroxide mix, Luna reasoned, touching her dark brown hair. She glanced in the rearview mirror and reminded herself, fifty in four days. Half-century eyes, nose, mouth, hair. Half-century ME. Luna smiled a little smile of self-mockery and put the window down a bit further. The sound of the ocean was turbulent and strangely tender to her, as the waves covered the entire beach, hissing and trying to reach the small cliff her car was parked on.

"Imagine boogie-boarding on that," Luna murmured, peering out to see if any brave surfers could be seen, but nothing—nothing, but the curve and foam of the immense waves. She'd bought a wet suit a few years ago, some flippers and a boogie board. Her granddaughter had asked, "Are you really my grandma?" Luna had laughed, hugging her, "Your mommy was my little girl. So, yes, I'm your Mamacita." Her granddaughter called her Tita, shortened from what she'd called her grandmother, Mamacita. Well, she can't speak Spanish, Luna understood, and Tita had a charm of its own.

Luna loved the thrill of catching a wave, hearing the roar behind her head, feeling it sweep her forward—shooting and flying through space. The immense power of the churning water, whiteness all around her body—the roaring sound, the surrender. And when she failed to ride the wave correctly and it pulled her under, angrily, with playful violence, she'd shoot up from the bottom laughing with defeat.

"Fifty years old, two marriages, two children, a grandchild, my new lover. Yes, my new lover. . . ." Luna realized she was talking to herself and stopped.

Her palm itched so much it burned, making her wonder if having her old dark brown hair color was worth it. She looked at her eyes: a lid lift? Her chin, her neck. . . . She held her left hand with her right hand and relaxed against the seat, her head tilted back. Luna thought of her grandmother, Isidra—her long, thick gray hair, the untouched face: beautiful. Her grandmother, in memory, remained beautiful.

"What would she think of my two marriages that didn't work out, my new lover thirteen years younger than me, my granddaughter, how she visits me from time to time. . . ."

Luna assessed herself, mentally, making herself not talk out loud, making herself not scratch her left palm. Why isn't my right palm killing me? Oh hell. . . . Okay, I've taught high school music for almost twenty-two years. I play the piano in an accomplished way. I give local recitals occasionally, classical to jazz. I'm considered eclectic. I stay in shape at the piano, I stay in shape physically at the gym, I run at the beach. Next I want to kayak and get rippling back muscles and slide through the silence far away from adolescent voices. Yet, I chose high school because that's when I began to enjoy my own kids as people, belligerent people, at times, but people *full of possibility*. Yes, I love to be in the presence of all that possibility, all that overflowing vitality and energy, even when it's going the wrong way, it's going, it's in motion because it has to be. It just has to be. To *be*.

A child from each marriage. First a boy, then a girl. Each marriage was supposed to work, and I loved them both differently, but with the same basic expectation. Now, I expect nothing that grand, everlasting love. Everlasting love, yes, that was it, I remember. If I walked out into these killing waves, what would be remembered, about me, that is: She was a good mother, stuck it through, a good teacher, played the piano well, a youthful fifty, nice hair, never had plastic surgery—my new lover would remember the other night, how tender we were with each other, my ex-husbands would remember only the formidable foe, isn't that what I remember. . . . No, think back, be honest, I always chose men with a sense of humor, so in the beginning there was large doses of humor, passion, pleasure. With Felipe, even the middle part was deepening and then it fell out from the bottom, no further, the end. Felipe, my second husband, my last husband, can't do marriage again, the battleground of everlasting love. . . . Why do men back away from intimacy, *knowing* the lover, at the end. . . . But would they remember *me*, the me I am, the me I meant to be? I did mean to be me, I did. I do.

"Why do I feel like a failure?" Luna ate her tears as they slid into her mouth. "Did I fail to become my possibility? The possible? I sure haven't found everlasting love. . . ." She switched to internal dialogue: My children live in different parts of the world and visit me, they continue to grow in their own right, they seem to love me, and I do love them, and my granddaughter, some friends, the old friendships became a mass of wounds, accusations. . . . failure, failure, failure, a relentless voice chanted in a soft, low-pitched voice. Why did I leave these people, why did they leave me? Because I couldn't continue to remain what I was in order to become. . . . Each year new students and they saw a new me, a better me, a braver me, or so I thought. . . . And the old students come back, some, because they remembered the *yes* I gave them, why can't I say yes to me . . .

My new lover, name him—Ron—do I love him, no, not yet—do I want him, yes—why am I patient with him? Because he's younger than me, because I don't expect everlasting love, because he hasn't refused me intimacy, yet, because he hasn't tried to master me, own me, resent me because I must remain myself. And what is this precious self if no one truly loves me, even with my children I refuse to lie down and play dead, I refuse to accept their confrontations, angers, judgments in a calm, motherly way. I cry, I yell, I fight them, but, oh, I love them, I do love them—but even for them I can't stop being who I meant to be, the me I am. . . .

Bobby—his name floated up—my intimate failure, my student who killed himself, who told me in a poem, with his eyes, that he wanted to be my lover. Bobby with the guitar and drums, so talented, so damned young, oh Bobby, when I heard, when they told me I was sorry I didn't give you that and I often wonder if that, that meeting between us, would've connected

140

you to life. The poem you wrote me, "To the Moon, Luna," I think my name seduced you, but like my own son I kept turning you back to life, your own life—I thought you were strong enough to take it, like I was strong enough to take it, my mother didn't, couldn't love me either, but, Bobby, little boy-man, I had someone who had strength like feathers in the beginning. . . .

Luna put her hand out to the cold, pelting rain and let it soothe her itching, burning palm. She looked out to the end of the beach and tried to remember Bobby's face clearly, his voice: "He used to smack me for almost everything. He broke my arm, jerking me around when I was around two, but he set it. He hurt me, he fixed me, the great doctor, admired by all. He smacked my mom too, but never in the face. She always drank a lot, who could blame her? When I was around ten he started punching me. When he broke my jaw I had to have surgery, so a friend of his had to do it and I told this guy what really happened. I told him everything, like I wrote it down and then the old man split, good riddance. But the old lady blamed me, Couldn't take it like a man, she said. I was just a kid and I was scared shitless. . . ." Luna took his hand, again, in hers and then Bobby's face disappeared. Why did I fail him, did I? You were supposed to go into life, Bobby, not death, not death. . . .

The next year she'd gone to Mexico for a year, alone, by the coast. She hadn't felt like a failure then; she'd felt set free, sad, but whole. Alive. She swam, sailed, slept outside her rented cabin sometimes, listened to Spanish, her own becoming fluent again. The eyes of the old women became Mamacita's, and Bobby and her grandmother became a single death to mourn. The warm, peaceful sea called her during the day and at night the Spanish became soft with music, intimacy, food. Her children visited her separately, as if to see for themselves that she hadn't gone crazy. Finding Luna dark with the sun, calm, changed somehow, they left, irritated and begrudgingly happy to see the mysterious transformation in their mother. Nothing dramatic, yet a shift in the compass had been accomplished, and their mother would go on. And they would go on into life, not death.

Yet, that year of release and transformation had been a gift from Bobby: his death. "Death into life into death into life, everlasting," Luna murmured, thinking of the music she'd composed in Mexico. "Pleasant, but not great. I'm no Mozart, that's for sure." No great scientific breakthroughs from this existence, no great poetry, I'll never be licked onto someone's monthly electric bill, so what, most people aren't. . . .

Luna rubbed her palm with the tips of her fingers—Don't scratch, she told herself, must be a leak in the rubber gloves. She thought of her mother dyeing her hair red into old age. Only during the last year did her hair emerge naked and gray. Luna had offered to tint it, but Carmen had said, "For who, the spiders?" As her hair turned, slowly, to its natural shade of gray, her face softened, but a harshness remained in her glance. Her shield remained intact. When they'd called her from the hospital, Luna realized, with her first sharp tears: I loved her more than I hated her, my mother. "Mother," Luna muttered. "Mother, daughter, wife, woman. Did I fail at everything?"

She opened the window wide, letting the cold rain sweep her. "I did my best, I did my very best. I'm sorry for nothing, except, maybe, Bobby." Luna closed her eyes and opened her mouth, tasting the rain. It was pleasant. Like being a child. She didn't care if she got wet or looked awful, like the year in Mexico, the year she'd returned to her childhood with Bobby's help. Wasn't that it, if I'd made love to Bobby we would've *both* lost our innocence . . . she opened her eyes. If he hadn't left the note, we would've thought the crash was a motorcycle accident, a slip off the highway, a moment of distraction, youthful stupidity . . . "I can't stand it . . . ." Is suicide a failure, is dying a failure—No, Luna answered herself, knowing Bobby, it took all his courage. . . . "Give my records to my old music teacher," and at the end, "See ya."

"See ya," Luna said, laughing softly. After the last divorce she promised, vowed, to not live, ever again, with a man who didn't love women. She'd been speaking to her daughter, woman to woman: "It's like this, I think, when you have self-hatred you can tolerate, well, even love, a man who doesn't like you, you know, a man who hates women. But when you begin to truly, I mean truly, love yourself, it's like your once-quiet, timid soul stands up and says, 'What the hell's going on!'"

Boy, am I realistic, Luna mocked herself—here I am still alone, more or less. I do have a few real men friends, and now Ron. I think Ron really likes women, at least he doesn't hate women. I think he still resents women though, hasn't gone through the long haul with the inner woman. . . . but I like what I've seen of "her"—"she" makes him interesting, a good lover, and his masculinity is still fresh and lovely. And me and my inner man, "him"—can't do without "him"; "he" makes me hum. I wouldn't even attempt to talk about this to Ron, probably scare the shit out of him, he's not ready, I mean he's thirty-seven and no kid, but I feel it, he's not ready, but maybe he will be, it's as though he wants to know and that's why he's drawn to me, but I feel if I laid that on him the next time we're laying there after making love, he'll leap out of bed and run out the door stark naked, screaming, "She's a fucking lunatic!"

Luna smiled at the thought of his lovely ass disappearing out her door. Actually, the thought didn't make her feel sad or anxious or abandoned. Not at all. It just, clearly, made her adjust her thinking in the light of reality, while acknowledging the presence of that possibility in Ron, if she waited. Maybe. Am I actually becoming wise? Luna laughed out loud.

Now, she formulated a clear and painful question to herself: In light of my possibility, *in the presence of my possibility*, am I a failure? Then her thoughts ran away with her: I could save no one, not really. I could only say yes or no and always in my own way, always, always in my own way . . . did I save myself for this, to be alone, what was so important, what was so goddamned important that I couldn't live without it? It.

How could Luna know that her grandmother had felt like a failure, that her magic had failed her, until that night she'd taken Luna to the stormy ocean. . . . how could Luna know the moment of failure is the magic moment. . . . when failure opens her mouth and weeps, singing. . . .

"I feel like a failure," Luna whispered. She put her hood on, snapping her raincoat snug and stepped out into the storm. Carefully, she walked down the slippery path to the sand. Then she heard it—a thin, high singing, then weeping, then singing. A chill went through her body. She remembered the stormy night with her grandmother, the night. . . .

Luna began to run toward the dark figure at the end of the beach, in spite of almost overwhelming fear. As she ran she began to weep without meaning to, saying, "Don't go away, don't leave me, it was all for you, wait. . . ."

She was tall, strongly built, and her wet cloak clung to her body. Her black lace shawl covered her head, shielding her unbearably beautiful face. She was neither young nor old. Her eyes were full of sorrow and peace. "Do you have it?" Her voice echoed the violent waves.

Without thinking, Luna opened her left palm and held it out to her. A small, star-shaped seashell glowed with an inner light. "Have I failed you?"

La Llorona began to laugh, softly, a subtle rippling in her body.

El Alma/The Soul, Two ❖

Luna stopped to take a photograph of a group of teenagers passing a joint around, but first she approached them, "Hey, what's happening?"

They looked like her, years ago, in her teens—dark-skinned, a little ominous, their eyes behind the sunglasses full of secret vitality: their anger. It fueled everything: sex, hunger, music, the blur of being. They smiled, exposing their teeth haughtily, "Not much."

It was almost sunset, and she'd have to work quickly in the fading light. She'd photographed a homeless family. Sitting with them around the small fire they'd built from scrounged wood—the older children, two boys and a girl, brought back scrap wood and unburned logs from an old campfire, paper from litter along the beach—Luna sat and talked with them as they ate their warmed hot dogs and cold beans from a can. The mother had said to Luna, "I know we eat better at the soup line, but sometimes we just need to feed ourselves. Pride, I guess," she'd laughed. "But tomorrow we go there for breakfast and there's school. All the kids got some good shoes from the bin just for school and pretty soon our number's up to get someplace to live and my husband starts a job next week. . . ." Luna had photographed her talking and smiling, feeding her baby diluted apple juice. In spite of her smile and hope, her eyes looked a hundred. The husband never spoke, but ate facing the ocean. The woman offered Luna a hot dog, and she'd declined saying she wasn't hungry, but the hurt on the woman's face, her gracious act refused, made her say, "Well, it does look good, everything tastes so much better by the ocean. You know, my grandmother and I used to come to the ocean just to have hot dogs. . . ."

I was only thirteen when he raped me, my mother's boyfriend, he was living with us, my grandmother dead, I was the cook, the housekeeper, everything my grandmother had done. Then, one night when she was at work, he came into my room as I was doing my homework, listening to music. "Hey, I'm still hungry, got any dessert, Luna baby, got anything sweet?" His eyes were fastened on me, especially on my almost-breasts. "There's some ice cream in the fridge, Larry," I said, keeping my eyes on my paper, on my homework. They were decimals or math or something, yes, decimals, like how much of you is left after someone takes your body, your soul, over and over, like that night, when I screamed so loud I thought the walls would explode, I thought the sky would crush me, I thought the earth would swallow me whole, I thought Mamacita's spirit would come back and grab him by the neck and shake him like the dog he was, breathing his stinking breath in my face, making dog sounds, hurting me, hurting me, then laughing at my tears, so I stopped crying and I stopped doing all the housework and I stopped cooking. I think after that night, and the others, all the other times, only .0 was left of me, or was it 0.?

My mother—was she my mother?—she believed nothing I said, calling me a lying little slut who'd suck a guy's dick for a nickel, and I'd never done anything like that. He made me do it and he paid me nothing. So, I stayed away from home—was it a home?—hung out with other kids like me, my friends, the other cholos. We did everything—well, wasn't everything *done to us*—we did coke when we were lucky, when someone had the bread, smoked grass to mellow out, lots of wine to paddle the waves, just float over the whole fuckin mess and laugh and laugh. Later I did shit, the stuff that kills you. I was tough, we were all tough, all of us, we were the free ones, no one fucked with us, and we fucked with who we wanted, meaning we didn't go to school no more, did a job now and then. I only started turning tricks, making them pay—I only sold myself to white men, her boyfriend was white—making them pay for me, and I thought each time they paid I got .1 of me back or was it 1.? I started fucking and sucking for money when my two kids were little and their father, one of my old cholo lovers, friend, ally against It, what kept pressing down on our sad-assed brown necks—It, the White People's System, the Men's System, the Welfare, the Food Stamps Line, the Housing Project, the Clinic where the

Doctors—were they Doctors?—never *looked at you*, the County Home where Mamacita died, where the poor, the unwanted, the homeless die because no one wants them, they're useless, they pee their pants, they see things, they burn stuff on the stove. *It* has no mercy if you can't placate It with $, lots of $, every day of your life, so when that cholo bastard started hitting me the way he'd seen his old man do it to his mother, I threw him out, my two little ones screaming and crying every time the police came, me bleeding. I started charging $ on the side—the Welfare and Food Stamps not enough to feed one healthy dog, that is if the dog wanted a two bedroom apartment in some Housing Project run by It and if the dog had to clothe itself and eat. So between the $ and the Welfare I placated It just a little, just a little for a while, until I tried some heroin, shot up just a little to forget It owned all of me, even the little (.) I thought I was. When I woke up, years later, in some cell screaming and sweating and shaking like I was dying, in fact I was dying, in fact I was dead. It killed me, even the little (.) was dead, my children were gone, my name was gone. I remembered my name one night, I mean really remembered it— when *they* said my name it was never me—when I looked out the window one night and heard a terrible weeping that seemed to be coming from the moon and it looked like a flood, like a tidal wave was pouring from the moon and in that woman's crying I heard music and my name, L U N A, like I'd heard it long ago, one night, holding my Mamacita's hand as we waited. . . .

They'd taken everything away, and I'd given everything away, I'd just given everything away, I couldn't fight anymore, all I could do was defend myself by disappearing, crouching lower, barely breathing, so when I heard my name in the moon's sad music and saw her tidal wave pouring back to earth, I knew that there was something stronger than It, stronger than all the Systems, stronger than what I always thought I was. Nada. Just a woman, a brown woman, an uneducated, junkie-woman, a raped girl-woman, a whore of a woman. Nada. But the moon said L U N A, loosing her tears, her flood, her music just for me, just for me, and, then and there, I got an inkling, just an inkling, that me, a nada woman, might be *todo*. Me, a todo, and I laughed, I really laughed for the first time like I had as a child and then, immediately, my laughter made me weep because my children were gone and I couldn't even remember what they looked like anymore . . .

A gringa, there in that place, talked me into going to a photo class, talked me into finishing high school, the GED, talked me into a computer class—she said to me once, that even though she was a gringa, It, the System, the Men's System she said, got to her too, that her father had raped her as a little girl, that she'd been an alcoholic, but she didn't lose her children like I did. She gave me books to read. One of them, *When God Was a Woman*, just made me laugh; I thought it was some kind of fucking joke book, like if you want a good laugh read this book—but it wasn't like that, it wasn't like that at all, it gave me that TODO feeling again like the moon did that night. This book was difficult to read, the words were hard and I had to use a dictionary a lot and sometimes I'd laugh right out loud because I, an uneducated—just to say that word, I, not the little one with the decimal at the top (i), but I, so proudly, no? I, a brown-skinned, junkie, whore, childless mother was sitting, thinking damned hard, over a book that was saying once there were people, *cultures*, all over the world, *civilizations* that *really* existed and worked for thousands of years and that these people saw the body of their Goddess, *the body of a woman*, and were filled with *reverence*, reverence, imagine?

Women *and* men filled with gratitude because they were *alive* because of her pussy where they came out, her womb where they were made, her breasts where they ate from; and over their temple doors, and sometimes just a simple gate to go through to a sacred place in nature, was the Goddess, crouching, with her pussy opened wide, like enter, leave, I am the gateway. Believe me, books like this and the other ones this gringa, Linda, gave me made me think and think and wonder if my brain could deal with all of this. Like another book talked about being a virgin wasn't about not being fucked, it's about being one-in-your-self, your own *self*, imagine? Like an old woman in her nineties with ten kids and lots of grandchildren could be a virgin, and if a woman *enjoyed* sex and had her share of orgasms, you know the clit thing, the pussy thing, the womb thing, *the whole body thing*, it truly made her a VIRGIN in the Goddess thing—AWOMAN, I say—get it, not amen—AWOMAN, to this virgin and Goddess thing, sometimes my TODO is so good I laugh *and* cry. Maybe I'm going crazy, I hope so . . .

Linda gave me poetry too—now, this was easier, the words were easier and it *looked* easier, but it could fool you because *suddenly* you'd realize what this poet was really getting at and your heart just bursts in your chest, AWOMAN, AWOMAN, AWOMAN, AWOMAN, like these words I memorized, they give me courage. . . . "I have been with you from the beginning, / utterly simple. / I will be with you when you die, / say what you will. / We shall never be finished. / This is possible, / a small gift, hush. / There is nothing I have not been, / and I am come into my power. / There is nothing I cannot be." And this book, *She Rises Like the Sun*, like the sun, imagine, it's filled with lots of women writing poems like this, women of every color in the same book. I'll never write a poem, but I can read, can't I, yes, AWOMAN, I can read. And I can take pictures like some kind of proof that I see and what I see is real and true and beautiful sometimes and ugly sometimes and funny and sad, you know, the whole thing, you know, TODO. . . .

I wonder if one of these kids are mine, this young one, this girl who looks maybe fourteen. They tell me my son died, an accident in one of those state facilities—I always imagine him being raped by the older boys and I can't help but think of who raped them, and I imagine him, my Ramón, suffering—Ramón, how I loved to say his name as a baby, RAMON, so strong, the R making you listen, RAMON, the sound of his name, the rolling R always made him smile and kick his baby feet, his feet that knew only air, ignorant of the streets, the System that honors no woman, the System that feels no gratitude or joy in being ALIVE, that feels itself dead, nada, and anything or anyone TODO makes the nada tremble, makes the nada hungry, makes the nada greedy—Ramón, I hope you didn't suffer too much, I hope you get a better chance next time. That's something else I'm thinking about, reincarnation—my Mamacita knew about that, my boy, my Ramón, was only eleven when he died, they say, and my daughter, Estrella, star to my moon, is alive, somewhere. . . .

"What's the camera for, man?" one of the boys asked, giving each word a clear, distinct threat to Luna's presence.

"I'm not a narc or a cop, just taking pictures of interesting people, like you, if you don't mind, and I'll send you a copy if you want one. . . ." Luna realized, with a buzzing in her ears, that she'd dreamt this moment last night, standing here talking to these kids. She'd thought, upon waking, that the dream was herself years ago, herself as an ominous, angry girl getting high with her friends, but, no, it's here and now. Her abdomen itched, or her solar plexus as Linda called it. She said it was a chakra, a center of energy and will like the sun. . . . "All I need is this chakra shit, Linda, come on!" Luna felt the itchy area begin to burn uncomfortably. She shifted her eyes to the sinking sun, the last light.

"How about it, guys, you look like me when I was a thug like you," Luna laughed. "I just didn't know how beautiful I was, man, I just didn't know and I want you guys to know, okay?"

148

"Sounds like a bunch of shit, but why not?" the youngest girl said. "Will you really send some copies and all?"

"Fuck, yeah, I promise! Would you please take off your sunglasses? Yeah, that's it, that's great!" Gold light streamed across their smooth, beautiful, brown skin and their exposed eyes were alive with defiance and, with a stab of pain and joy, Luna also saw playfulness. Playfulness, she realized, these children just want to play, to be innocent in their hungers, their desires and, oh, fuck, to be loved, to play, to be a child, to have a soul, to be a virgin in your soul after everything that can happen to you happens to you . . .

Luna shot rapidly, hoping to get at least four or five good ones. They joked around, leaning into each other. One of the boys took his girlfriend into his arms and cupped her breast, laughing, and the girl looked straight into the camera without any shame.

"Hey, Francisco, she don't want no porno, let go that tit!" one of the boys yelled.

Luna laughed with them as they continued to play for her camera, like the dream, until the sun gave no light.

As she walked away from the group, after taking an address to mail the photos to, she smelled the sweet smell of grass and a part of her wished she could go back and join them just for a toke or two, but she knew she couldn't. Luna told herself, Woman, you're going to be fifty in two days, fifty fucking years old and she laughed out loud, but she felt lonely, suddenly, very lonely.

The beach stretched out in front of her and darkness was beginning to hide things from her eyes. Common sense advised her to go back to her car and go home. "Shit," Luna muttered, walking on. The burning sensation in her abdomen flared up, making her walk faster. She folded her arms over her abdomen, protectively. "Me, a fifty-year-old fucking virgin, me and my goddamned chakras."

Luna stopped and looked out to the moving water and then up to the dark sky. A slim, translucent crescent hung in the darkness and glowed. She sank to her knees facing the sea and the crescent, watching the thin, delicate path of light move toward her on the waves. "My poor, innocent children, my babies, I failed you, how can I pretend it's not true—you, Ramón, did you play, and you, Estrella, mi Estrella, did you shine?" As she wept she heard another's weeping, close by, and then she heard a faint music. The burning increased, making her double over.

"Do you have it?" a beautiful woman's voice sang with the music. Terrified, Luna looked up and saw what her mind had erased from her childhood memory, from that night she'd held out her hand. . . . She was still unbearably, unbearably beautiful, and Luna was relieved to clearly see what had frightened her as a child—her beauty was so complete, so perfect, so filled with TODO, with every human possibility, that her beauty teetered on the edge of terror, of beauty's opposite, ugliness. She was neither young nor old and her eyes held a playfulness as she sang again, "Do you have it, Luna?"

Luna looked up into that terrible beauty, that indescribable face, that todo, but what comforted her, what encouraged her was the playfulness in the night-sea eyes. "I've failed everyone and I have nothing."

A searing pain in her solar plexus made her clutch herself tightly and cry out. Then, she felt a hot coolness in her hand and there it was, the small star-shaped shell burning with its own inner light. Reluctantly, Luna held it out to La Llorona.

A peal of laughter like music, like a child, rang out from La Llorona's perfect mouth as she bent over to cup the burning star-shaped seashell with both of her hands, warming them. "Ayy mi Luna," she sang, "ayy mi Estrella. . . ."

❖ El Alma/The Soul, Three

Luna sat, wedged, between her favorite dark rocks, facing the North Sea. During medical school she'd come here so often she could've sworn the nearly black rocks called out to her, Luna, Luna, come and sit, be with us, your only family, us, the dark, dark stone, us, the dark ones. . . . She heard them whenever they came into view, when she turned away from the boats, the people. At first, she'd stayed just a few minutes, sitting on a lower rock keeping her feet in the coarse sand. It was so silent, so forlorn. Now, she sat in a kind of rock-chair nestled between the large, dark stones, and she had to remind herself when it was time to go.

Tomorrow was her fiftieth birthday, and she knew her lover and friends were planning a huge party. Yes, of course, she was loved, very loved. Now. Her lover, Mara, they'd been together for nearly eight years (Mara with the gold-green eyes, Mara of the sandy blonde hair, Mara who knows my soul, my secret: that I killed and I'm not sorry. No, not ever).

It was thirty-seven years ago when Luna locked herself in her room. She could hear them laughing and drinking, the music on very loud. Mamacita died the year before, and now she let him live with them. Luna waited. She waited for the laughter to turn to screams, Dolores' screams. Whenever they drank he beat her, then he'd make love to her. Make love, Luna thought, can you call that making love? No, that's making hate, there *is* a difference, I know there is. . . . Her thirteen-year-old mind clung to this

151

fragile thought. Even when they do it, it sounds like he's hurting her, only mixed up with her greedy pleasure. . . . Luna heard the first slap and her mother's cries. She wants it that way, she wants it that way, oh Mamacita, stop them, stop them, stop it from happening again, not again. . . . Then the next slap and the next—her mother began to scream. Luna felt for the big butcher knife—Mamacita had given it to her just before they took her away: "Hide it, sleep with it, niña, no te dejes, nunca, niña, cabrones. . . ." Luna remembered the soft, loose skin on Mamacita's hands, the feel of feathers, her eyes like an old captured eagle. Fierce and sad at once.

Luna felt the long, hard steel, and the silvery coolness comforted her. The screaming stopped, and she waited for the sounds of their hate making. She listened to her grandmother's words, "No te dejes, niña, nunca, nunca. . . ."

Then she heard the front door slam shut, and there was silence except for the loud music. Luna got up and peeked through the curtain covering the little windows on her locked door. He was leaning against the wall, without clothes, swearing and talking to himself.

When is my menstrual going to stop, Luna mused. Fifty and still menstruating, but no hysterectomy for me, the doctor. I must admit, I rather like my uterus. I imagine it talks to me. When I met Mara I was cramping, just like today, and she said, "Yes, mine talks to me always." Ha! What would my male colleagues think of that? Who knows, maybe some of them, secretly, speak to their penis. These cramps, I'll go in for a massage tomorrow, with the party and all. I wonder where they'll have it? That they've kept from me. Luna sighed with relaxation. Tomorrow's my day off and my birthday—no children's faces, illnesses, the ones born with addictions, in such pain, the ones dying of cancer, the ones dying of AIDS. . . . These are my children, my uterus told me, leave me empty and you will have more children than I could ever create. I did as she told me and, of course, it's true. How often I thought, Mamacita would be so proud of me and that thought kept me going even when I felt like an outsider, a foreigner, backward, stupid, an unrepentant killer. . . . but didn't that act, as Mara made me see it, force me to be a healer. . . .

He fell, crashing, against the door but the lock held. Then he twisted and pulled at the doorknob, rattling the door back and forth, making the small windows quiver. "Open the fuckin door, ya little bitch, know yer in there, ya little slut, jus like yer fuckin mother, c'mon Loonie, I jus wanna stick it tya's all. . . .

Luna dressed quickly and stood behind the door, terror exploding in her ears; her heart, an insane machine, made so much noise she was afraid he'd hear it and grab her and hit her and hurt her and make her and make her like her mother, make her. . . . but her hands didn't even tremble as they held the knife. Both of them held the knife as she'd seen it done in the horror movies. It makes sense, she reasoned in a flash, if I'm going to stick this into his body I'm going to need all my strength. . . .

Her heart wouldn't be silent; it was the loudest sound in the world. . . . "Don't let him hear it," she murmured. "No te dejes, niña, no te dejes. . . ."

He broke a window with his fist and turned the knob; blood ran down the door onto the floor. "Fuckin spic bitch, alget ya fer this!" He clutched his hand and staggered toward the bed where Luna had bunched her pillows beneath the blankets. As she stepped from behind the door he turned, saw her and lunged. The knife moved with precision, with a life of its own. She saw blood on his face, throat, chest, and he never screamed or made a sound. He simply fell. . . .

Dolores testified on Luna's behalf and the court declared her an unfit mother. A woman who Luna cleaned house for petitioned to legally adopt her. She and her husband were from Denmark. They sent Luna to their relatives the next year to get away from San Francisco, The Trauma as they called it. "No one will know in Denmark," Demerce said, holding her. "You'll be a brand-new person. You'll be able to do anything. We'll visit you and you can visit us. Luna, you'll love my sister and already she loves you, hearing how brave you are. Oh Luna, at thirteen I had a loving father and a loving mother. Let us do this for you, yes?"

Dark-skinned, dark-haired, dark-eyed, she'd arrived to live in a household of light-skinned, light-haired, light-eyed people, but they succeeded, finally, in making Luna feel special and beautiful because of her difference. They encouraged her to take Spanish as well as Danish, to remember her own language, and they even learned some Spanish to speak with her. At her birthdays they bought her piñatas and the rest of her adolescence went by uneventfully. She was often startled by the peace and calm of her life, and then she'd wait for the horrible to find her, and when it didn't she felt free for another stretch of time. At last, she didn't feel like a foreigner or stupid, and, when much later, as a doctor, she guarded and saved lives, she didn't feel like a killer. . . . Nunca, niña, nunca. . . .

It was nearly sunset, and Mara would be at the restaurant in an hour and a half. Luna swept the horizon with her eyes, letting the long, northern twilight soothe her. In her twenties, when Luna began to openly see women, her family finally understood her perplexing disinterest in boys that marked her teens. It was hardest for her aunt, but she got over her hesitations and invited Luna's lover to family get-togethers, dinners, the Sunday picnics. When Luna joined a Wiccan Circle of Goddess worshippers, they added a small statue of the Tibetan Goddess, Tara, to their mantelpiece.

Who could ask for more? I've been so lucky in this life of mine. Fifty? I hardly look into the mirror; instead I look into Mara's beautiful, loving face or into one of my children's faces.

"These damned cramps!" Luna hissed with irritation. "Shouldn't the absence of these, at the very least, be the privilege of turning a ripe old fifty?" She laughed at herself. I really do love my blood to come, she thought, if only it'd come without cramps like these. I'll have to do a series of acupuncture again, that certainly helped. Luna put both hands over her uterus and closed her eyes. I wonder what childbirth would've been like, to have a child. . . . Mara was willing to be pregnant for us, but I never was. My uterus kept saying, No, stay empty, full of *your* possibility, let the other children find shelter there—and then Mara and I decided not to have any personal children. Luna smiled. We're each other's children and children of the Goddess. We're each other's mother, who could ask for more?

Luna felt a fluttering in her womb, a muscle spasm. She imagined it was a small fetus, a barely stirring fetus. She concentrated on her cramps and thought, briefly, of the six-year-old black boy with the immense hazel eyes, her favorite child, who was dying of AIDS. Tomorrow she'd drop in on him in the morning, early, and bring him the large box of color crayons she'd promised him and a dinosaur coloring book to surprise him. Then I'll have to get out of there and not linger and go for my birthday massage.

Birth day. Day of my birth. The woman who bore me, Dolores. Mother. My unmother. My mother. My dead mother. I forgave you long ago, in fact, I forgave you that day you said I killed him because I was only defending myself. You told everyone there, in spite of your obvious humiliation, what he did to you, what you let him do to you, how you left me alone that night, how you drank, how you stayed with him knowing his cruelty and violence, how you said, "What else could she do with a man like that?" And when you began to cry, your horrible sobbing, I wanted to hold you and comfort you, but I couldn't, I couldn't reach you. My arms never did reach you. It was too late, mother. And it was too soon. I was only thirteen and then I came here to be a brand-new person and I gladly left you behind.

Tears fell freely down Luna's face, and, just as suddenly as they'd started, they stopped. "Thank you for my life, Dolores. Who could ask for more? Wasn't everything for this moment, for who I am? You wrote me and I didn't answer you. I failed to reach you, mother." Then it struck her as though it came from a blind spot she'd never considered. . . . Maybe I'm not a healer, maybe I'm just a doctor, a cold technician, after all. . . .

Her hands over her uterus felt suddenly hot as the cramping increased. Then she heard the small, soft, distinct voice of her uterus: "Killer and healer you are whole." Luna doubled over, kneeling in the sand. . . . "Killer and healer you are whole," her burning womb chanted with a sweet urgency.

"Do you have it?" a woman's voice sang.

Before Luna looked up she knew who it was. She looked deeply into the eyes that held immeasurable strength, that instantly flowed into immeasurable tenderness, to strength, to tenderness. . . .

A tearing pain in her vagina made Luna cry out and her hands knew what to do—she caught it. Filmed in a delicate membrane of blood was the small star-shaped shell. It pulsed with light.

Luna cradled it, weeping with unleashed joy and La Llorona laughed with utter delight. She took her black lace shawl, which shielded her face, and wrapped it around them both in a large, graceful movement, to protect this wholeness, this birth, from curious eyes.

"A mother you've become, a mother you've become to death and to life," La Llorona sang as she cradled Luna in her infinitely powerful, protective arms surrounded by the lace of night.

"Wasn't everything for this moment, for who I am?" Luna murmured.

La Llorona laughed and continued singing, "A mother you've become to death and to life. . . ."

El Alma/The Soul, Four ✛

Luna walked from her campsite onto a disappearing trail surrounded by the silent, eerie, immense sand dunes. She could see the wind's design—the design of their dreaming, Luna thought. Maybe this is where our dreams are truly recorded, then swept away for new dreams to come. She felt like writing, but decided to wait for the ocean. In her pack was pen and paper, lunch and wine.

"Alone and loving it!" Luna shouted to the risen sun. Tomorrow the poetry reading at Sonoma State, the next day a poetry panel. Funny how the critics and scholars can give the illusion that your work is important, even if you make very little money. The money's in readings, the occasional permission to publish, grants if you're lucky, or if you're a Ph.D., piled higher and deeper, or a white-male-professor-type, and I'm neither. "Me and my little exclamations to the world, ha!"

Today's the day, the big one, the five and zero. . . . the mountains this winter seemed harsher, though not enough snow fell. . . . maybe that's it, the lack of snow. But I was invited to Stanford for a symposium of women poets, poets of color—how about bleeding women poets of color turning blue, purple, from shouting into the wind. . . . but the people in the audience, those select and discriminating people that actually read poetry and drive cars, pay bills, get married, get divorced, have a few favorite TV programs, but still love the language of the soul, that varied, tortured, exquisite, brutally beautiful language of the soul—when those people respond, clap, *get it*, I get it. . . .

The whiteness of the sand made Luna watch her feet move, made her look down, concentrating on her legs and feet. As she moved further away from the campground, the silence and isolation became more apparent. The feel of her knife in its leather holster, strapped to her waist, was reassuring; she had a good repertoire of Kung Fu kicks and punches and a couple of death blows if she needed them. Instead of age making her cautious, it was making her *dangerous*.

Luna wondered what she must look like: Do I look fifty, do I look like someone's grandma, do I look like a poet, do I look afraid? Her movements were confident, but not showy, which was exactly the antidote to the lurking coward: The Rapist. They don't want a fight—belly up, belly up, they pray.

"You know where it started," Luna murmured. That boy in the park and no boy or man ever hurt me again and got away with it, not even the men I've loved, not even my sons. I never elicited their protection, I never received it, so the love I got, was it freely given. . . . was it . . . is it . . .

The heart of a dangerous woman, what would it look like? Luna mused, smiling at the thought. At fifty she could think it; at twenty she would've apologized profusely. A dangerous woman's heart: Luna saw a soft, red, bloody, life-giving muscle pierced by long, slender cactus thorns, and each thorn a story, each thorn a face, a pain, a pleasure. Some of the longest, most graceful thorns had been placed by her mother when she was very young, maybe four years old, and then throughout her childhood, they grew shorter and finally stunted. Then, her grandmother, Mamacita, planted her long, graceful thorns so carefully.

Some of the stunted, short, thick ones surely came from her mother's cruel and violent husband. Luna's stepfather had taught her the value of being dangerous, the unpredictable: "That girl's a witch!" she'd heard him say after she knocked him out cold one night, and later when she knocked out one of his teeth with her twelve-year-old fist and ran to the phone to call the cops. There wasn't a trace of fear or guilt in Luna's eyes, only sheer satisfaction. "That girl's a witch!" How could he know he'd given her the words she'd needed; how secretly pleased she'd been with her new status of *witch*.

And the longest, most slender thorn had a blossoming violet flower with translucent tips—this was her grandmother's death. Luna could see her grandmother on the empty church stage, even the preacher's podium gone, the stage very plain, very bare. This was no ornate Catholic church, just a simple Spanish-speaking Baptist church; no altar, no tabernacle. So, when Mamacita came out to recite poetry she became the altar, the tabernacle—to see her, Luna remembered. Where was the old, brown woman with pain in her bones, in her joints, with the bad lungs, with trouble controlling her bladder, with no money, with stockings that tended to fall around her knees, the slow walk, the sorrowful eyes, the misplaced old Indian woman who should've never left Mexico, who in everyday life had to fight for the dignity to cash her welfare check. . . . where was that old woman? In her place was strength and vision, yes, danger. She who had healed with her medicines and stopped in this country because some called her *bruja*, witch. When the poetry rolled from my grandmother's mouth her back was straight, her beautiful gray hair was long and loose, down to her waist. . . .

As Luna crested a dune, the sea came into view and with it a lovely, fresh gust of wind.

. . . her eyes were shining, shining, burning, because she looked out at us and *saw*. And her voice created silence; her voice made people weep, remembering what they, too, once saw. Luna stood facing the sea and shut her eyes. In the darkness, the violet flower blossomed deeper, more translucent. Her dream-eye itched as it often did when she wrote, and she scratched it absentmindedly. The translucent tips of the violet flower became rays of extending lights, extending into death, into infinity. Sometimes the flower was a deep red rose with a light-filled center, but the flower, in whatever form it came to her, was born, always born, from her grandmother's death. Her infinity became mine, yes, of course, when I rushed into that puke-green hospital room, refusing to believe she was dead, and then she raised her head and her eyes *saw* me and she spoke her last poem and it became mine. "Luna, no me quiero morir, nunca, nunca. . . ." She chose infinity, consciously, the blossoming flower.

The tide was out and the shoreline held no human footprint. It could've been a million years ago or a million years ahead. The sea is perfect; Luna let the silence fill her. The sun is perfect. Dare I think it—the day is perfect. "Knowing everything that I know, the raped women and girls in El Salvador, Guatemala, Turkey. . . ." She remembered the story of the sixteen-year-old girl in this month's Amnesty International newsletter, who'd been tied to a cross and raped, tortured, brought down from the cross, and raped again. ". . . . the abuse of our children, the abuse of our Earth, all of it, all of it, in spite of it, I say to this day, you are perfect and I have *seen it.*" Tears of joy fell freely from Luna's eyes. "That's what Mamacita saw in me, in the Earth she loved, the little flowers, perfection. That's what she *saw* when she looked out at the people in the church and recited poetry—perfection—and that's why they wept, because they *remembered*."

Luna scanned down the beach, up into the sand dunes and it was clear. She stripped off her clothes and ran, full speed, into the chilly water screaming, "Perfection, perfection, perfection!"

Laying full to the sun and shivering, she asked herself a familiar question: What if I never published again? Would it be enough to write and exist in my own life? Without the tiny audience of readers and scholars, the obscure poetry panel, the historical babble of, Art is the mind of culture. . . . Literature is the conscience of culture, etc., etc. Would it be enough to exist in the sun's warmth? Who would actually miss my little exclamations? Really, Luna, she told herself, a Professional Poet? Maybe if your role were Shaman, Oracle, or even Temple Prostitute, there might be some value in it. Value.

She imagined not going to the scheduled reading and symposium, and she knew what would happen. She'd be replaced, effortlessly. Then, why do I publish and read and write these little exclamations, why? A deep, intense itch made her rub her forehead, her dream-eye. She thought of getting pen and paper, but the idea of writing depressed her. She thought of her lunch and wine, but it was still too early.

The day is too beautiful, too perfect, to waste on this puny shit—so no one gives me grants or genius awards to live on, so I'm not distinguished enough to be a visiting writer, so I don't hold a people together, and if I do glimpse the future who listens, so I'm a failed Professional Poet, so what?

Laughter pierced Luna's silent tirade. Then the words, "Do you have it?" Luna jerked upward to a sitting position, instinctively covering her breasts. She was comfortable with nudity, but whenever she returned to the populated areas her old caution and forced modesty surfaced: fear. In the mountains she and her friends often swam nude in the river and lakes. She'd come to the conclusion that her body wasn't bad for fifty. It had a secret: sensuality. But she wasn't prepared for what she saw—the most perfect woman she'd ever seen. Her body was dark, her legs were full and strong, her pubis a lovely, dark triangle, her belly slightly rounded, her breasts high and gently sloped, her neck erect and graceful and long, black hair fell to her waist covering her shoulders, and over her hair a delicate, well-made black, lace shawl floated in the wind as though it were a part of her hair. Her face was fully revealed in the sun and her skin was dark and healthy. Her eyes were the exact color of the sea at that moment—a pale bluish green, almost transparent with light. It was as though she saw through you with the power of the sun. Her cheek bones were high and her mouth was lush and full, smiling with eternal self-satisfaction.

What made Luna gasp was what her eyes were telling her as they laughed with joy, yet containing the knowledge of her sorrow, alternating somehow, yet filled with this moment, this perfect joy: *I know you are.*

"I know I am," Luna said out loud. A blinding light in the center of her forehead, in her dream-eye, made her shut her eyes. She saw a blindingly brilliant, star-shaped seashell. Luna began to reach for it, but the woman caught her hand and stopped her. Her touch was gentle, yet unmistakably firm, unyielding.

"So, I'm stuck with it, is that it? I thought you wanted it back?" For an instant, Luna thought she'd cry, but the day really was too perfect, the day was truly, truly perfect . . . and she began to laugh at the absurdity of her task. With her small exclamations she was to make people remember, and she knew it would always come to this—yes, she would kill for it and that was the dangerous part. She'd killed so much of herself to come this far: a sometimes paid Professional Poet, naked as the day she was born, holding hands with her perfect sister, Death, Muse, Goddess. Her perfect Mother who knew the angle of every thorn in her dangerous woman's heart, and who wept with her.

Now she laughed with Luna as they ran, full speed, into the sea. As the first wave engulfed them, Luna knew she was gone. Her eyes were shut tight against the salt and the star burned brightly making her see La Llorona's face, her body, her sunlight eyes, clear as a dream.

"I know I am. I am the granddaughter of a woman who in her eighth month of pregnancy, pregnant with my mother, saved her husband's life. He was to be buried alive by Pancho Villa's men for an article he wrote about their rapes in the small towns. She threw herself into the grave and begged for his life. She refused to leave the grave, her with her full-moon belly, so the men accompanied them to the U.S. border. I am the grand-daughter of a woman who, when asked the contents of a sack by a U.S. border policeman, quickly emptied it, blew it up, popped it, and shouted, 'Aire mexicana, cabrones!' I am the granddaughter of a woman who re-fused to return to the country she loved because she'd been forced to leave, leaving forever the graves of her four infant dead. I am the grand-daughter of a woman who took my side when I hid from my uncle. I was five years old, under the table. When he reached for me, I stabbed him with my blunt baby scissors—I made him bleed. I am the granddaughter of a woman who spoke her truth in the face of her death. I am the daughter of a woman who refused the old ways to live in the new ways, who got me drunk on screwdrivers when I was fourteen and my labor began—we walked to the hospital, laughing—her medicine was laughter. I am the great-granddaughter of a woman who was known for her healing powers—a woman who married five times, each time a better man. She was an undefeated Yaqui Indian. She was a bruja, as was her daughter, my grandmother."

Luna dove under a light-filled wave and emerged spitting water, laughing. "I know who I am."

She ran for her towel. She dried her hands and reached for pen and paper.